TOM BLUEFOOT, WYANDOT SCOUT,

GENERAL "MAD ANTHONY" WAYNE,

AND THE

BATTLE OF FALLEN TIMBERS

Lloyd Harnishfeger

Order this book online at www.trafford.com
or email orders@trafford.com

Most Trafford titles are also available at major online book retailers.

Printed in the United States of America.

ISBN: 978-1-4907-5424-6 (sc)
ISBN: 978-1-4907-5423-9 (e)

Trafford rev. 01/21/2015

www.trafford.com

North America & international
toll-free: 1 888 232 4444 (USA & Canada)
fax: 812 355 4082

BOOKS BY LLOYD HARNISHFEGER

HUNTERS OF THE BLACK SWAMP

PRISONER OF THE MOUNDBUILDERS

THE COLLECTOR'S GUIDE TO AMERICAN INDIAN ARTIFACTS

LISTENING GAMES FOR PRE-READERS

LISTENING ACTIVITIES FOR BEGINNING READERS

LISTENING ACTIVITIES FOR GRADES 3 – 4

BASIC PRACTICE IN LISTENING FOR GRADES 5 – 8

THE KID WHO COULDN'T MISS

BLACK SWAMP WOLF

TREASURE ON BEAVER ISLAND

FOREWORD

The following is a book of "historical fiction". Dates and places are as accurate as research can establish them. Known historical figures, such as General Anthony Wayne, Chiefs Little Turtle, and Blue Jacket are represented as accurately as present day history portrays them.

Supporting characters, activities, conversations, and other such "invented" materials used to move the story along are offered in ways the author feels certainly could have happened.

Readers can rest assured that they have been given at least a glimpse into this important time in the history of America.

Finally, when delving into written history of any and all past events, always remember the following quote, attributed to Napoleon Bonaparte: "History is a lie, agreed upon!"

"Blue Foot ya call yerself? Wal I calls ya 'Stinkfoot!' You redskins is all alike. Thieves, drunks, murderers, I don't care if you are supposed to be scoutin' for the General. Yer nothin' but trash to me, so what you gonna do about it? I'll fight you any way you choose. Tomahawks? Guns? Knives? Or jest plain fists? You choose. Or are you yella as well as red?"

Tom Bluefoot knew it was useless. Big Cas was half a head taller and a lot heavier than the skinny young Wyandot. He circled, keeping well out of range of the big militiaman's muscular arms. A growing circle of General Wayne's soldiers jostled for position, better to see the show.

"Give it up, Tom!" yelled red-headed Sean O'Casey, a soldier and Tom's only friend among the whites. "You've got no choice. He'll kill you sure if you fight him."

"Shut up Red!" a soldier shouted. "Let Big Cas take care of the red devil. We don't need him or any of his kind scoutin' for us. They're all spies anyhow. Get him Cas!"

Tom's hand inched toward the knife sheath on his left thigh as he continued to circle and keep his distance, his eyes locked on the big man's face. He was very afraid. Even should he be lucky enough to win this fight, the other soldiers would soon finish him off anyway. A proud man, Tom Bluefoot considered his chances. They were bleak.

"Watch it Cas! The sneakin' redskin's going for his knife. Get him! Use your 'hawk. Kill him before he gets his knife out. We'll clear it with the General." There were shouts of agreement from the watchers, as they crowded ever closer to the combatants.

"You know that ain't true," Sean yelled, trying to get in front of Big Cas. "He called Tom a bad name."

"Shut up, Red! You always was a Injun lover. Let old Cas finish this worthless redskin. What you waitin' for Cas? Use the ax!"

Pride, honor, courage. All had been hammered into the young Indian since he was old enough to understand. It was plain enough that closing with the soldier would mean a quick death if he was lucky, or a slow, painful end from his wounds if he was not. What would Black Pipe, perhaps watching from the Spirit World, think of his nephew if he refused to fight? These thoughts rushed through his brain as he saw the tomahawk sliding slowly from the sling under the big soldier's left arm.

Suddenly Sean leaped, crashing into Big Cas' side. Two militiamen grabbed O'Casey by his red hair and threw him to the ground. It all happened in a second, but it was enough. Tom whirled, slipped through the circle of men and sped into the forest, leaping logs and bushes like a frightened deer. He knew that no one from the troops could ever catch him. He was free and out of immediate danger, but even as he flew ever deeper into the forest he felt humiliation and shame. Was he then a coward? Would he run from the enemy when the coming battle was joined? What was the Spirit of Black Pipe thinking of him at this moment? Had his long dead uncle been able to see what had just happened down here on the earth?

Fatigue was setting in, and he slowed to a fast trot, still traveling in a generally southern direction, guided by the rising crescent moon.

Tom used all the tricks he had been shown to avoid pursuit. When fallen logs favored his direction he raced along them, then at the end leaped far to the side. Twice he reversed his direction for nearly a mile, following his own back trail. Pursuit by any of Wayne's soldiers did not concern him. They would have lost his tracks less than half a mile from camp! No, what brought the lingering terror was the probability that several other Indian scouts, be they Wyandot, Miami, Shawnee, or of other tribes would be sent after him. Certainly they would not be long fooled by his attempts at deception.

Fatigue finally overcame his fears and he dropped to the ground. A pile of leaves had drifted in beside a large rock. He made this his bed.

Sleep was overtaking him when The Voice began. It seemed to originate in the rock itself, but Tom suspected it was only from inside his head. The words, if that's what they were, matched the rhythm of his pounding heart and heaving chest.

"DISGRACE! SHAME! COWARDICE!"

"I must agree with the truth of these accusations, Uncle," Tom stated miserably. "I ran from the enemy without even attempting to fight. But remember the story you told me once during that extra cold winter? I can hear your voice as if it were yesterday:

"three wolves had surrounded a young bear. They had injured the bear's back legs a little, but not enough to cause real damage. Of the three, the most bold bragged to the others that he would get the bear by the throat and bring it down. He tried, but bravery was not enough. The bear killed him with a single swipe of its paw. When the second wolf, a female, joined with the bigger animal it bit her across the back. She managed to crawl away, but she soon died as well. What should the only living member of the three now do? What is the difference between courage and foolhardiness?"

Black Pipe did not answer his own question. He had finished speaking.

Somewhat comforted, Toom-Shi-Chi-Kwa, "he who paints his foot" whom the soldiers just called Tom, curled up to sleep.

An angry red Jimmy squirrel wakened him just before dawn. At first light the young Indian did a silent circle around his resting place. Nothing was disturbed, and no tracks were in evidence, so Tom was certain that he was in no immediate danger from pursuit by Big Cas or any of the other soldiers. He returned to the boulder at his sleeping place, sat down and composed himself. “Perhaps,” he mused, “Black Pipe will visit me yet again. I need guidance, for I don’t know what I should do now.”

Tom Bluefoot sat in silence for some time, but there was no word from Black Pipe at all. Perhaps he had dreamed the whole thing. He considered his options. Basically he had three. Return to chief Little Turtle’s camps along the My-ah-mia [Maumee] river? This was out of the question of course. He was so hated there because of what he had done that a horrible death would certainly be his fate. Another option would be to stay hidden in the forest and try to make his way back to Fort Pitt and the Quaker family who had bought him from his Wyandot father. Such action was not even worthy of consideration. He had no food, no weapons, not even an ax, and his former home lay nearly three hundred miles through the wilderness to the northeast.

The decision was clear enough. He must return to General Wayne’s army. Once there he could attempt to contact his friend, Sean O,Casey or one of the Wyandot scouts while still staying hidden from the murderous Big Cas and his cohorts. It would be difficult if not impossible.

He tried once again to contact the spirit of his uncle, but was unsuccessful.

At first he considered approaching the camp at night, but soon discarded this plan as too dangerous. With only a crescent moon to see by he would make too much noise. A nervous sentry, patrolling the perimeter, would certainly shoot on sight any approaching Indian!

Heaven help him if Big Cas was on guard duty when he made his attempt! There was no real choice however. Tom gritted his teeth, stretched his muscles, and began the long walk back toward the American army camp.

He was amazed at how far he had come on his mad flight the night before, but finally well toward sundown, he heard the ring of axes straight ahead. He crept forward until he saw movement along a little creek. There appeared to be a squad of six or eight soldiers cutting wood. Out of sight further ahead, another group could be seen pushing a hand cart loaded with water barrels. Tom had no choice but to show himself. A bearded soldier lunged for the musket he had left leaning against a tree. He threw the weapon to his shoulder and took aim at the Indian. "Hold on, Jake!" yelled a grizzled older soldier who seemed to be in charge. "He ain't armed and he ain't no bigger than a flea. Don't shoot him. Not <u>yet</u> anyhow."

Tom raised his hand, palm up. "I'm a scout for General Wayne," he intoned, not moving. Looks of amazement followed his greeting. They had not expected to hear him speak in their language.

"A scout are ye? Where's your gun then? You got no kit, and Little Turtle's braves are hunnerts of miles from here. You ain't no more scout than me! Keep him covered, Jake. We better tie his hands and take him back to camp. The rest of you-uns keep on getting the wood. Give him a prod, Jake. <u>March,</u> young feller!"

"What do ya think we ought to do with him, Zeb? I sure don't intend to bother old 'Mad Anthony' with another stray Injun. That General's too handy with

His cat-o-nine-tails! I seen that half-breed, Meechum, get about thirty lashes, jest fer talking back to a sergeant. We better be careful."

"Our best bet is to take him right to the command post and turn him over to the lieutenant there. Let the officer decide. But you know, the General might want to talk with this redskin at that. Him being able to speak English good, and the varmint skulking around our wood detail in broad daylight. But anyway that's for the lieutenant to decide. Keep moving there, you! What's your name anyway?"

"Toom-Shi-Chi-Kwa."

"Like hell it is!" Zeb bellowed. His hand flashed forward and struck Tom on the back of the head. "Now we know you can talk English goodern me, so give us your real name, not that redskin gibberish." He turned to Jake. "Them 'breeds allus has a English name to use when it suits them. So what is it, you?"

"The soldiers call me Tom."

"Tom what? That other mish-mash had more to it than just 'Tom', so don't give me that!"

"Tom Bluefoot."

"Your foot's no more blue than mine is, so I don't believe you at all. If you lie to us once more I'll tell the lieutenant to give you ten licks with the 'cat'. So what do you say now?"

They continued the westward march for another hour. Tom said nothing, but fortunately they were finally in sight of the camp. Several militiamen looked up in surprise as the little procession moved among the tents toward headquarters.

Tom secretly scanned the troops, hoping desperately that Big Cas was not in sight. But he was! The bully and four others were preparing their supper over a small fire. Tom and his captors were nearly out of sight when one of the soldiers suddenly shouted, “Hey Cas, there’s that redskin you scared off yesterday! Looks like the wood detail grabbed him.”

All five abandoned their supper and ran to intercept the procession. Cas planted himself in their path, folded his arms and demanded to know the details.

“We caught him while we was cutting wood. We’re taking him to the lieutenant. The General may want to question him, but we sure as shootin’ ain’t gonna bother old General Wayne! Let the lieutenant do that. That’s what them officers gets paid for.” All the soldiers laughed, except Big Cas.

“I’ll take charge of him,” Cas stated, still standing in their way. “He attackted me yesterday, then run off like the coward him and his type all is. The General won’t want to bother with no skinny redskin, scout or not. We can handle this here sitiation ourselves. Leave the lieutenant out of it.”

“Nope Cas, we caught him and we aim to take him to Wayne’s quarters ourselves. Knowing how you got a case against him, we understands that, but he’s our prisoner now, since we’s the ones as captured him. So stand aside and let us past.”

Jake was amazed at Zeb's bold remarks. Big Cas was known to most of the camp as a dangerous man when challenged. Caswell took a step closer and towered over Zeb and the prisoner. "You can come along if you want to, sure enough!" Zeb said hurriedly, backing up a few paces. "Sure! You come right along with us. Maybe the lieutenant will want to ask what happened between you and the scout."

"Wal I'll sure tell him!" Cas blustered, but he gave menacing looks at Tom's captors. He didn't think any of these soldiers had actually witnessed the fight, but he was taking no chances. "You all knows that redskins is all liars anyway. Ain't that right?" No one answered. "I said ain't that right?" Cas roared. They kept on walking but several grunted in assent.

Tom's steps faltered, which earned him another prod from Jake's gun barrel. His fortunes were bleak enough even without Big Cas' lying testimony. The small scout had learned to be a realist. Who would the lieutenant believe? An Indian's word would mean little when opposed to those of a soldier in Wayne's army. He plodded on, trying to ignore the shouts and taunts of those soldiers not on duty.

General "Mad Anthony" Wayne's command post was situated on a half-acre of hard-packed clay just east of the Sy-ow-Tan [Scioto] River. His tents were larger than any of the others, but otherwise not elaborate. The procession approached warily, uneasy in the presence of so many officers. They halted a few paces from the General's quarters, unsure how to proceed.

"Where's the lieutenant?" Jake whispered, glancing around at several soldiers of various ranks.

"He's gone back south to the Ohio. General Wayne's orders," a nearby sergeant stated. "Who wants to know? You better not bother the General unless it's mighty important. He's in an even worse mood than usual! Supplies ain't been coming in. Little Turtle's braves are the main reason why. They've been hitting our supply trains real regular. Can't catch them at it. They just hit and run. Of course they take horses and anything else they can carry away. It sure don't make the General very happy! That's why he sent Lieutenant Staley to see what's holding things up. I sure hope he can get some answers. We're all 'walking on eggs' around here because of Wayne's bad mood. If I were you I'd hold your business up for a couple days, or until things settle down a little."

"Thank you Sergeant," Cas said sweetly. "We shore preciates the advice, but see we got a Injun prisoner here we thought we should bring to you officers' attention."

"That little one there? Why he's no bigger than my twelve year old son back in Marietta. How'd you catch him anyway? Took a whole regiment I reckon! Haw Haw!"

"Took him without firing a shot, we did," said Zeb. "We was on wood-cutting detail and caught him sneakin' around our camp. So we grabbed him and here he is."

"Oh my, the General will just love to have you bring this little redskin into his tent. He really needs to spend an hour or two trying to get the truth out of this illiterate no-good! After all, Wayne's got nothing else to do, just trying to keep everything straight, discipline about fifteen hundred loud-mouthed fools that calls themselves soldiers, keep all of them fed, hang a few deserters, teach 'em to march, and . . . Wait! Here comes General Scott. He's General Wayne's Second-In-Command. You can tell him your story, but mind my advice. Stay out of General Wayne's way!"

"What's going on here, Sergeant? What are these recruits doing at headquarters?"

"Sorry sir. I told them not to bother General Wayne. They've got a prisoner they thought might be important. That's him, the little Indian with his hands tied. Claims he's a scout. They're all just now leaving."

"Beggin' your pardon sir," Big Cas spoke up, "we wouldn't think of disturbing our commander with just any redskin scout that we re-captured, but this one's a troublemaker and a deserter! We all knows how this army takes quick care of deserters! So we brung him in. Shoulda shot him right away I reckon but we thought we was doing right."

"I am no deserter!" Tom cried.

"Well I'll be. . . that one speaks English I see. Bring him over here to me."

They dragged Tom to the Brigadier General and pushed him forward. His eyes were wild with terror. Everyone in the campaign knew the fate of any deserter from this army. Tom himself had witnessed the hanging of two young men, still in their teens, who had run off but had soon been caught. The troops had been mustered and forced to watch what happened to any who chose to run. The two had protested their innocence, tears streaming down their faces, but those near enough heard their necks snap.

"Well men it looks like we have to interrupt the General with this problem. He gave strict orders that he be informed of any desertion taking place in his army. He probably won't need more than a minute or two for this anyway."

"I am not a deserter," Tom intoned pitifully. "This man, Big Cas, and some of his friends, called me names and started a fight with me. I had no weapons and he was going to kill me. So I ran into the woods. I planned to return, and was on my way back when I was captured by these men."

"How long were you gone then?" the Brigadier asked, obviously not buying Tom's story.

"Over night is all."

The Second-In-Command turned to Big Cas. "This Injun says you started the fight. Is that true?"

"No sir. It sure as hell ain't!" Cas roared. "He's lying just like all of them does. You can't believe a word they say. Lying, stealing, and getting drunk, that's all you can count on with any of them red devils! I don't see why we have to have them in camp. What do we need scouts for anyway? Half of them is spies, which I think this one here is too," he whined.

"You better watch your mouth, Cas! If the General heard you questioning his polices it would get you ten lashes 'well laid on" with the cat-o-nine tails!"

"Yes sir! I meant no disrespect sir, sure and I didn't. I leave them kinds of plans strictly up to the officers and I never interfere with anything. Just a common soldier doing my duty, sir, and that's God's truth, sir!" Cas pleaded, greatly alarmed. "You won't say nothing will you sir? I meant no . . . "

"All right! We'll see if General Wayne will sort this out. Just the scout and you three men come with me. The rest of you shirkers quit gawking and get back to your duties. You two; what are your names and ranks?"

"Sir, I'm Jake and he's Zeb, both privates. And he's Big Cas, or I should say Private Caswell."

"Zeb is it? Just a private? How long have you been soldiering? You look old enough to be a captain by now!"

Zeb grinned. "Well sir I was a sergeant once. Served with General Washington at Valley Forge. That there was a bad winter for sure. We was all either freezing, starving to death, or both, so some of us decided to take a little vacation!"

"So then you were a deserter too, were you?" the officer demanded angrily.

"Well not erzcakly. My enlistment was up. Had been for two months but we wasn't allowed to leave. General Washington's orders." When I came back that spring my enlistment time 'cut no ice', and I was busted down to private. I never put in for no rank after that. I'd had enough of that there! I'm happy being just a plain old soldier in this man's army, Sir!"

At the command tent even the Brigadier General hesitated for a moment before clearing his throat and asking permission to enter.

"Wait five minutes then present yourself, IF you have something important to discuss," General Wayne shouted in his rather high-pitched voice. He could then be heard talking normally with several others inside. General Scott hurriedly marched Tom, his two captors, and Big Cas several yards away from the large tent's door flap.

"The General's gout has been acting up again these last few days. If he's got his foot up on a chair or something, in heaven's name don't bump into it or we'll all feel the lash!"

They waited, unsure if they would be able to see the Commander at all. Five minutes stretched to half an hour .

"General Scott, Sir, mebbe we ought to just forget this whole thing," Zeb whispered. "It's getting on to night and maybe Wayne ain't had his supper yet. I know I ain't, and a hungry man can get mean if he ain't et!"

"Be quiet! If you let your mouth run on like that when we report to General Wayne you'll be put on report," General Scott growled, pacing nervously back and forth.

"Sorry Sir, but like I was sayin' . . ." Zeb's mouth snapped shut in mid-sentence as the tent flap opened. Two junior officers emerged, talking quietly to each other. They saluted the Brigadier, but paid no attention to Tom and the privates.

"You may enter if you're still out there." Wayne's voice carried well from within the canvas walls. They trooped in, Brigadier General Scott leading the way.

The General's foot, swathed in bandages, was indeed elevated, resting on a wooden crate. "Mind my foot!" Wayne ordered, glaring at them. "Well, what is it Scott? Any word from Lieutenant Davis? Has he managed to learn anything about the supplies we are supposed to be getting?"

"No Sir. Sorry Sir. Not a word yet, but we're hoping he'll get back by tomorrow. I'm sure we'll have a favorable report from him the moment he gets back Sir."

"Well we'd better get a 'favorable report', Wayne retorted. "If we don't have those supplies soon, we'll be a mighty poorly equipped army! And a hungry one as well."

"Sir, I'm confident that General Washington, I mean President

Washington, won't let us down. We'll get our supplies, I'm sure."

"Who are these men?" General Wayne demanded, looking them over. "What's an Indian doing here? State your business. I have a great deal of work to do yet tonight." They remained silent as he fumbled to light the candle on his small portable desk.

"I too have much to accomplish yet this evening, General," Scott said. "So with your permission sir, I'll leave these men to give you the necessary details."

"Dismissed." Scott backed hurriedly out of the tent and disappeared, feeling greatly relieved.

"Well somebody say something. Who's to be spokesman for this detachment?"

Cas stepped forward, saluted, and began. "Sir, allow me sir, to do the talkin' seeing as how I'm the one as knows all the details on this here matter."

"Well go ahead then. Speak at will."

"Thankee Sir. Well the reason we come direct to you sir, is we knowed how you hate deserters, and this here Injun is one! Sir!"

"I assume this Indian is one of our scouts, Is that correct?"

"Yessir it shorely is. You've got right to the matter at hand sir!"

"I have little time, private. Give me the whole story from the beginning and be quick about it."

"Certainly sir. Well this Injun, who claims to be one of our scouts, started a fight with me over nothing at all. So I offered to fight him fair and square, any way he chose, in order to settle the matter in the ranks. That way we'd save taking the matter to the Adjutant," said Caswell self-righteously. "But like all of them red devils he was a coward and run off in the woods. We'd have never seen him again, ceptin these soldiers here caught him and brung him in."

"I'm not a deserter!" Tom muttered.

"What's that? You speak English, do you? Tell me why I shouldn't hang you right now. How'd you learn English anyway?"

"I was brought up by a Quaker man. My Indian father had a problem with liquor. He sold me to the Quaker to get money for strong drink."

"Are you going to tell me you didn't desert yesterday?"

"I did run away, but it's not like he said at all," Tom said pointing at Big Cas. "I didn't start the fight, he did. Called me a name and said all Indians should be killed. He was going to fight me, but he had a tomahawk and a musket. I was unarmed."

"You lying varmint," Cas yelled. "You was drawing that knife and meant to get me with it. I wish you had, 'cause then I'd of got you fer shore!"

"Be quiet! There will be no further shouting during this enquiry. Now were there any witnesses to this altercation?"

"Yessir, there shorley was, sir. About six or eight of my boys seen the whole thing. Want me to go and fetch them, General?" Cas asked eagerly.

"What do you mean 'your boys'? Do you have rank enough to command a squad of men?"

"Well not erzackly you might say, beggin' your pardon Sir, but these are good fellers. Four of them was in my regiment at Stony Point. We fought the redcoats side by side during the Revolution. Been pretty much together ever since. They look up to me sort of, Sir!"

"You were at Stony Point? Under whose command?" General Wayne's demeanor had changed dramatically.

"Why Sir we was in your very own regiment! Remember that bayonet attack you ordered? That there was a victory were it not Sir? We licked them good, we did. They never knowed we was comin' but they shorely found out! Ain' that the truth General?"

Tom felt the weight of imminent defeat. Not only was his enemy a legitimate soldier, but he had also been in a battle under General Wayne's personal command!

"You know private, I think I may remember you in that fracas. As I recall there was another Kentuckian even bigger than you. Am I correct in this?" Wayne asked.

"You are, General! You shorely are. Cartwright his name was. Avery Cartwright. We used to rassle for the troops to watch. We was pretty even but I always won in the end. He was lucky to die pretty quick, Sir."

"Lucky? If he was shot, how could that be considered lucky?"

"Beggin' your pardon Sir, but on account of he was gut shot! I seen the wound. Went in right through his belly button, it did. He could have lasted for days but he didn't. I'd say that's lucky General."

"We'll talk more at a later occasion, Private." He then fixed his eyes on Tom. No mercy could be observed in his demeanor. "What do you have to say for yourself Indian Tom?" he asked. "We've heard nothing from you as yet. Speak up!"

"As I said sir, I'm no deserter. Big Cas called me 'stink foot' when my real name is Toom-Shi-Chi-Kwa. It means 'he paints his foot'. The men just call me Tom. Tom Bluefoot. Caswell said all Indians are liars and thieves, and that the army would be better off without any Indians around, scouts or not. Then when some of his friends gathered around, he said I could fight him or he was going to kill me where I stood. Either way I would lose. He was drawing his tomahawk to finish me. All his friends were urging him to do it too, so I ran. I intended to come back later," he finished lamely.

"You intended to return did you?" General Wayne said, his voice heavy with sarcasm. "Do you have anything else to say in your behalf?"

Tom could almost feel the burn of the hemp tightening around his neck. He knew the situation was hopeless. For an instant he had a wild impulse to dash from the tent and head once more for the darkening forest. Reason told him it was an impossible plan. He felt numb. His brain seemed to be frozen. What could he do? Wayne hated deserters, as was well known. Now the fact that his enemy, Big Cas, had taken part in the Patriots' famous victory at Stony Point meant General Wayne would be even more inclined to believe the bully's lies.

"So you have nothing more to prove yourself innocent of desertion before I pass sentence upon you?"

Black Pipe's voice suddenly seemed to speak in Tom's addled mind: "Remember the wolves and the bear!"

In a voice hardly above a whisper, Tom Bluefoot, Wyandot scout, finally answered the General. "My uncle's name was Black Pipe," he began. "He not only taught me the ways of the forests, but also how to conduct myself when in peril. One time he told me the story of three wolves attacking a bear. Two were killed. The third, knowing he could not win the fight, ran away. That is what I did when Private Caswell and his friends were about to kill me. That was why I ran, General."

"So your uncle saw no dishonor in running from a battle? I thought you Indians put such great store in courage, even to the point of death. Isn't that true? Your uncle gave you bad advice, young man!"

"Do you have anything more to say? I'm very busy and this problem is taking far too much of my time."

Tom felt he might have one last chance. He spoke again. "General Wayne," he pleaded, "Private Sean O'Casey saw the whole affair. Could you take time to call him and hear the truth of what happened?"

Big Cas immediately blurted in. "Beggin' your pardon Sir, but I wouldn't waste any more of your time on this here deserter, Sir. That there O'Casey he's talking about is a bigger liar than this Injun is! What's more, him and this Injun is friends, so you can bet he'd lie to protect his friend. Also, I think I heard a cavalry officer send that red head and some others off to get hay for the horses. So he'd be hard to find in the dark, Sir, so like I said I'd not send for him. He ain't needed atall!"

Wayne considered Caswell's remarks, then fixed his gaze on Tom once more. "I'll grant you this favor just to be fair, but not tonight. Corporal Makely!" he shouted, "Come in here."

The man must have been eavesdropping just outside the tent, for he stepped in almost before the General had finished speaking. "Place this man under guard for the night. See that he has something to eat. I'll see all of these men first thing in the morning. And one other thing. Find a Private by the name of O'Casey and have him here at first light."

As Tom was marched out, his hands still tied, General Wayne nodded at the other three. "See that you're all here too. Dismissed!"

With no guardhouse available, Tom was simply shackled with leg irons, one leg on each side of a caisson wheel. The cornbread and beans still lay beside his blanket untouched. The very thought of food sickened him on this night which he felt sure was to be his last. Sleep also was impossible. He prayed for some sort of vision. When none came he angrily kicked at the wagon wheel.

"Lay still, redskin!" the guard muttered. "You wake me again and you'll feel my boot in your backside!"

As the night wore on, almost in desperation Tom sought the God of his foster father, the Quaker, Eli Miller. Tom remembered the evenings when Eli had read to him from the large black book that lay on a table in the main room. He was slowly learning to drop the "thees and thous" the old Quaker used. The troops had found his use of these words hilarious. "Hey Injun, talk a little Quaker for us! Are thee hearing us? Dost thou want anything?" the quaint terms seemed always to reoccur in times of stress.

Tom knew how to contact Eli's God, but whether the "Three Part God" heard him or not he could not tell.

At first light the guard removed Tom's shackles. "If you try to escape I'll blow your heathen head off!" He shoved the barrel of his musket against Tom's neck. "You know," he said, "If this here gun should go off, accidental like, We could save the General a whole lot of trouble!"

That was frightening, but he had to ask himself if a ball thorough the throat would be better than a hangman's rope. Like a shroud, complete despair settled over him. He peered around. Where was Sean O'Casey?

"Did you sleep real good Injun?" Big Cas crowed. "Ready for a little 'necktie party'?"

The tent flaps suddenly opened. "Was that your voice I just heard Private Caswell? Come in, all of you. You know, Caswell, I've been thinking of the campaign at Stony Point, and your part in it."

"Yes Sir! Them was the days, wasn't they?"

"I've also been thinking of your friend. The one who was bigger than you."

"Sir! Yes Sir! He was a big one alright. Him and me used to rassle. He was good but I always won out. We had a real bust-up right before the Stony Point battle."

"Just before the battle started? What time would that have been?"

Big Cas' eyes narrowed a little. "I can't recall erzactly, it bein' near five years ago, but maybe just before chow time?"

"Private Caswell, you are a liar and a fool. You made up this story to ingratiate yourself with me!"

"But. . . but . . .General . . I . . . that is . . ."

"The entire engagement began a little after midnight! Hearing this ridiculous fabrication cannot but cast doubt on your account of the fight with this Wyandot scout. Officer Conley! Find a Private named Sean O'Casey!"

"Perhaps," Tom thought, "I won't be hanged after all!"

"Untie his hands," Wayne said.

"But Sir . . . Beggin' your pardon sir . . .you gots to let me . . ."

"That will be all, Caswell!" He had not used the designation "private"!

At that moment Lieutenenat Conley arrived, Sean O'Casey with him.

"Private O'Casey reporting," Sean stated, standing ramrod stiff.

"At ease, Private. Do you know these men?"

"I know the scout, and this man, Caswell."

"Did you witness a fight between Caswell and this Indian?"

"I did Sir."

"It wasn't no fight atall!" Big Cas growled. "This thievin' Redskin attackted me for no reason. Then he run off in the woods. Deserted, he did Sir!"

"Is that the way it happened?"

"No Sir. Thou can ask Sean what was the truth. He tried to stop Big Cas from getting ready to kill me."

"Scuse me, General. O'Casey is a poor soldier. Everybody knows he's as bad a liar as that there Injun!"

"That will be all, Mr. Caswell!"

Cas hung his head, but remained silent.

"Begin at the beginning, Private O'Casey."

Sean spoke fast, but his account was thorough. When he had finished Wayne seemed satisfied.

"Orderly!" The General called, "collect a detail of five soldiers and shackle this big man to a tree beside the drill field."

Cas blanched. "Post-shackle me?" he whispered. "I ask you to show mercy. I couldn't help what I done, Sir. I hate all Injuns, and I reckon I got a little carried away."

"So you hate all Indians? Do you realize that scouts like Tom Bluefoot are absolutely necessary to the success of this campaign? As it is, Chief Little Turtle, a man we know little about, commanded two recent battles which resulted in the defeat of our American forces. We need relevant information on him before we close with his warriors."

Despite his clear order not to, Cas spoke again. "I can tell you all you need to know about the murderin' devil! He's a liar like all of 'em are, Sir. He and all the rest of his kind need a good killin'!"

"I will ignore your violation of my direct order to remain quiet. You may speak at will."

"Thankee Sir. The main reason is them murderin' savages busted into our cabin just before dark. We thought we heard turkeys gobblin' in the woods. I grabbed Pa's gun and run out to get us one. They wasn't turkeys, they was Injuns! I stayed hid while they done their dirty work on my family. They tomahawked Pa, and dragged Ma outside in her nightdress and shot her full of arrows. Sam tried to boost my little sister out the window but they busted his head open with a war club. They smashed the baby's head in, and took my little sister, Clemmie, she was just ten year old, set fire to the cabin and run off. I run back and went in. Got burnt." He pulled up his shirt to show an ugly purple scar. "I won't be sayin' what they might be doing to my little sister now, but as for the baby, Sarah her name was, I found her poor little body all chopped up and layin' half in the spring. I could go on, General, but I'll just shut up."

Wayne said nothing for a moment. "I see," he said at last. "There are too many stories like yours these days. I plan to finish the Indian problem. May God will it to be soon!"

"General Wayne, Sir, reporting with the prisoner escort."

"I'll take my punishment like a good soldier Sir, but let me say this much. You give me a good rifle, not a musket like the troops has, and put me in the front line of battle and see if I ain't the best Injun shooter in this, man's army! A liar I am, Sir. But give me real good gun and let me at them varmints and you'll not regret it, Sir!"

"I'll see that you get your wish, Caswell. Your marksmanship will be sorely tested! Tom Bluefoot, I will speak more to you over vittles."

Tom left the tent in a daze. Sean walked beside him, grinning. "You probably won't be hung," he said, "but I doubt if the General is going to forget about what he considers desertion."

*   *   *

Big Cas stepped along smartly, head up and shoulders back, doing everything he could to show he wasn't afraid. A suitable sapling was found on the corner of the drill field. Sweating in the hot sun, most paid little attention to the man being led to the tree. They had seen other men at this same spot. Cas watched them. For the first time in his army career Cas wished he could join them!

"Sit down, big guy. Scoot up to the bole of that there maple."

"How about a blanket and some water?" Cas whined.

"Hold your horses! They'll be coming. Maybe after chow time. Besides, you won't be needing any blanket until tonight when the skeeters come out! Haw, haw!" As the escort left, one turned and yelled, "Have fun, but don't go anywhere!"

Back at the command post, Tom sat in a pool of shade within sight of the General's tent. It was after mid-day when a private hurried up. "The General will see you now. Mind your manners in there! His gout is giving him fits!" General Wayne had loosened his blue outer jacket and removed his hat, but other than that he seemed totally unaware of the sweltering conditions in the tent.

"What is your actual Indian name? Did I hear you say it was Toom-She-chi-Kwa, the literal meaning being Tom Bluefoot? Is that correct?"

"It means 'he paints his foot'. My mother named me, as is the custom of the Wyandots. I never knew exactly how she came to call me that. As you already know, the men just call me Tom."

General Wayne appeared more relaxed than usual. Apparently the supply train had been located and was on its way. "Did you say you were raised by a Quaker family?"

"Yes Sir, that is true."

"Then how is it that you find yourself scouting for the American army?"

"My father, a Miami under Chief Little Turtle, drunk again, decided he wanted me back with him. Probably so he could 'sell' me again for more money for the white man's liquor."

"So the Chief of the Miamis is Little Turtle?"

"Sir, his real name is Tenskwatana. As you know this can be translated as Little Turtle in your language."

The General stood up so suddenly his camp stool fell over backward. Looming over Tom Bluefoot, Wayne asked urgently, "Did you ever spend any time in Little Turtle's village?'

"Only about two years Sir."

"Two years?" Wayne exclaimed. "Did you ever have any opportunity to observe Chief Little Turtle?"

"Observe? I do not know that word."

"Of course. Did you ever hear him speak?" He was leaning so close to Tom's face it took all the scout's will power to keep from reeling backward.

"My father was drunk whenever he could get liquor, so I spent much time with his older sister. Her lodge was but a short distance from the Council House.

At night we would crawl up to the wall and hear the speeches. We were often caught, but never punished for this."

General Wayne, deep in thought, did not speak for some minutes. Tom stood obediently at attention. "Did you ever see soldiers coming to these meetings?"

"Many times, Sir. They were British, and sometimes Canadians. They all had swords hooked onto their belts."

Wayne did a good job of controlling his excitement. "Did you ever hear the names of any of these soldiers, Private Bluefoot?"

"No Sir. Oh, there was one who came sometimes from Detroit. I think he was called McKee or Magee something like that. He always brought presents!"

"Your words give me much to think about, Tom Bluefoot. Report to me again at sundown. Dismissed."

Tom left the tent deeply dejected. Hanging, the Native Americans firmly believed, could cause the spirit of those executed in that manner to wander the earth for untold ages!

Once again under the same shade tree, Tom considered his chances. While it seemed that Wayne wanted any information Tom could supply regarding Chief Little Turtle and any involvement of British troops along the Maumee, realistically, Tom felt that he knew very little that could be of help to the General.

Toom-She-chi-Kwa stood up, casually dusted off his leggings and looked around the camp. No one seemed to be paying any attention to him. Escape during the daylight hours was futile, he knew. Several Indian scouts were in camp and would track him down in minutes. Night would not work either. Now was the time! A bullet in the back would be a better way to die than choking his life away swinging at the end of a rope!

He moved slowly toward the forest, keeping his eyes to the front. Terror suddenly seized him when a soldier ran toward him, shouting for the lieutenant.

"He's running away, Lieutenant! There he goes!" Two other soldiers joined the first, bringing their muskets to bear. "One more step, Indian, and we'll shoot you dead!" Trembling all over, Tom stopped and did not take another step.

Major Rickers burst out of the Command Tent. "Don't shoot that Indian!" he yelled. General Wayne's orders!" Tom was saved, at least for the moment. In minutes he found himself shackled to the same caisson as before. Beyond terror, he noticed that General Wayne himself was approaching. Without his tricorn hat and minus the scarf he appeared somewhat less intimidating. But not much!

"So you were planning desertion again were you?" he roared.

Tom remained silent. What could he say?

"Answer the General!" Major Rickers snarled.

"It is true." Tom whispered. "I do not wish to be hung by the neck. I would rather the soldiers shoot me. No one believes me. Only Private O'Casey, and he is somewhere else."

"I had not decided what your fate would be, but now you have given me no choice. Have him at my quarters after evening mess. I will be at the parade ground."

* * *

What is this man doing with a rifle?" Wayne demanded, peering angrily at Big Cas.

"Sorry Sir, but I can explain why we done give him a gun for."

"I'm waiting."

"How about if I gets the sergeant over here? He can explain it better than me."

"Good afternoon, General Wayne," the sergeant said, "this is a unique situation we have with this particular prisoner."

"It certainly must be!" Wayne intoned dryly.

"Well sir, this man kept bothering the sharpshooters. He claimed he could outshoot any one of them if he was given a rifle like they were using. He just kept it up until we was all sick of hearing him, so I gave him the piece . . .and . . . he. ."

"Move this ridiculous account along, sergeant!" Wayne growled, folding his arms.

"Well General Wayne, the upstart was this man outshot every one of the sharpshooters, even still shackled to that tree!"

The General spent some time observing the marching, then returned to the prisoner, Caswell. The Commander procured a rifle, and held it for a moment. "Major Rickers," what would you think of giving the troops some entertainment? I'm thinking of a shooting match."

"An excellent idea, General," Rickers agreed. "It would do much for morale."

"Release this man and give him a rifle," he said, watching critically as Big Cas staggered erect. The soldier examined the weapon at some length.

"Is the rifle not satisfactory, Caswell"

Cas saluted smartly then answered, "Well I sure does thank you, but this ain't the same piece as I was shootin' before. If we're gonna have a shootin' match I want that same gun agin."

"One gun is the same as the next, is it not?" Wayne was getting impatient.

"No General, they ain't. That one I had before pulled a tad to the left. It took me two extry shots to make sure."

The troops were allowed to sit in the shade for the marksmanship contest. Big Cas seemed little concerned about the outcome of the coming affair. Four troopers, well known for their prowess with a rifle, were selected to take part along with Caswell. A square of old buckskin, a black circle in the center, was to be the target. One of the shooters stepped off seventy-five paces and nailed it to a tree.

Cas stood, casually watching each of the men as they loaded and fired. The four chosen soldiers' efforts were indeed impressive. Wayne smiled in approval as all but four shots struck well within the target. He had divulged nothing of the strategy he planned to use against Little Turtle and Blue Jacket, but a large part of it was to deploy sharp-shooting snipers on the front lines of battle.

The braggart, Caswell, was the last shooter. He steadied the rifle, aimed carefully and fired. His first shot cut the edge of the black bullseye. The next two were within it! The watching troops howled, enjoying their fellow soldiers' embarrassment. Big Cas faced the watchers with a triumphant smirk.

Wayne approached the soldier and extended a hand. "Well done, young man! Well done indeed!" To the Major he said, "Do not re-shackle this man. He has earned his freedom!"

"Thankee kindly, Sir! Uh . . General Wayne, Sir . . ."

"Yes, what is it Private?" Cas grinned at the apparent re-instatement of his rank. "Could I have a word with you, private like?"

Wayne turned to those standing nearby. "Excuse us gentlemen."

"Permission to speak, General?"

"Granted. Please be brief."

"Yessir! Well it's about that Injun. Tom somethin' or other he calls hisself."

" What about him? He has attempted to desert once again, and is now awaiting my interrogation."

"Aha!" Cas crowed. "I knowed he would. That's why I wanted to talk to you."

"Speak up, man! My duties are pressing these days."

"I think he's nothing less than a Injun spy! Think about it. He claims he was bought and raised by whites, then got what you might say unbought by his Injun dad. This puts him back in Little Turtle's camp. Then he shows up here, speakin' English like a lord. He'll claim he can go back there and bring you information about the Injuns' plans. The question is, what kind of information will he be giving to the redskins? And while we're at it, that red-headed private, name of Sean, well I heard him planning to give water and vittles to the prisoner. That's 'giving aid to a prisoner' ain't it?"

"Thank you. That will be all," Wayne said shortly. Cas peered after him, frowning.

*　　　　*　　　　*

"Tom! Hey Tom!" a familiar voice whispered. Sean slipped under the caisson. "I got you some water and a hunk of venison. Better gobble it quick before we both get caught."

"I thank thee, Sean. Thou art a real friend!"

"What's to happen next, Bluefoot?"

"Sean, you better get away from here. You're in real trouble for helping me. I'm to meet at headquarters. I think General Wayne is going to order me to be hanged for desertion."

"Surely not, Tom! But I hate to tell you there's more bad news. I thought you should know."

"What is it this time?"

"It's Big Cas. He's telling the General that you are a British spy!"

"Well Sean, one thing's sure; they can only hang me once!"

Sean slithered backward until he thought he was safely away. Tom hid Sean's tin cup in the weeds behind the wagon wheel, and lay back down, covering his face with one arm.

"Looks like you got yourself in a heap more trouble, Injun!"

Tom was not surprised to see Big Cas sauntering toward him. "I gave you a real helping hand with the General. Bet you don't know what I told him about you."

"I know alright. Thou hast made me out to be a spy. I joined the army to scout for the Americans. I want them to win the war so all this killing can finally be over."

"Old Wayne ain't going to believe a word of that. I told him what you was probably up to, and I could tell he was thinking about it real hard. I suppose you heard that I won the rifle contest. I figure now he'll give me command over a squad of good shooters if we ever finally get in a scrap with old Little Turtle and the rest of them murderin' devils. Course you won't see any of that. It's hard to see anything while you're swinging from a rope! Haw haw"

"I am not afraid." Tom said, but he was trembling all over.

"One reason I can shoot so good is account of my really good eyes. I can see lots of things, Injun Tom. Like I seen a certain red-headed soldier sneakin' around here with a hunk of meat and a tin cup. I think I'll just go and see the General. He'll be mighty interested that I seen that fool bringin' aid and comfort to a prisoner!"

"Don't do that Cas. I'm begging you! He just felt sorry for me. You don't need to tell General Wayne about it. It was only a cup of water and a little venison. Please?"

"Beg me all you want. It was your kind who butchered my family and dragged my little sister off to God knows where. When I get the chance to shoot Injuns I'll be the happiest man alive! Now you just stay put. You hear? Haw haw!"

* * *

"There's a man here who says he needs to see you, General. It's the big man who won the shooting match."

"Ah, yes, Caswell I believe. I have no time for him. We'll be marching north at first light. Dismissed."

Caswell had the idea that the General was now almost his friend. As he helped the sergeant bring the food, he told the man about Sean O'Casey bringing food to the prisoner.

"I doubt if General Wayne will be interested in that story right now. They're planning another attack on one of the Indian villages."

Muttering angrily at the rebuff, Cas trudged back to his tent. No one was foolish enough to ask him any questions!

Pain shot through his ankle and into his shin. He couldn't help a stifled groan at the pain. "How will I ever force myself to mount when we march?" he asked himself miserably. "As if the previous defeats of our armies, the desertion of some of my troops, and the raiding of our supply trains were not enough, I must be cursed with this 'thorn in the flesh' as St. Paul put it in the Scriptures."

He forced himself to lift the elevated foot from the packing crate, doing his best to ignore the pain. Carefully rearranging the coat he had used to pillow the throbbing appendage, he reached for the small jug of rum. Never a heavy drinker, the general turned to the jug in hopes that the liquor might help numb the effects of his affliction. He did not realize that the occasional use of the sweet beverage was a part of the very problem!

The big private, Caswell was it? had mentioned the battle of Stony Point. As the rum warmed his stomach, Wayne's thoughts drifted back to the year of 1779. Since England was then at war with the French, the Revolution was finally going better. He smiled in spite of the pain as his thoughts swirled back to that third year of the American Revolution.

* * *

The midday heat settled like a fog upon the waiting troops. General "Mad Anthony" Wayne sat his horse and surveyed the lounging soldiers with a critical eye. He paid special attention to the light infantry company, comprised of top level troops recruited from various regiments of the regular army.

The unit had been put together for this very campaign. They were mostly silent, the way battle-hardened soldiers usually were before combat. The rest, however, chattered nervously among themselves, or walked aimlessly about, trying to appear unconcerned about the coming battle.

Wayne was very proud that George Washington, Commander of the American army, had granted him the privilege of commanding the battle for the British fortress of Stony Point. He had pledged himself to complete victory, and would settle for nothing less, which was undoubtedly why he had been given this assignment.

A major British army had routed the skeleton crew of less than fifty Continental soldiers. They had been forced to retreat. The loyalists hauled seven cannon up the crag, and with these secured, felt well in command of that section of the Hudson River.

The plan of attack had been drawn up by General Washington himself. He had observed the fortification of the site, and was well acquainted with what would be necessary for its capture. He and [then Brigadier] General Wayne conferred often, and it appeared ever more possible that a surprise attack in the dead of night could result in a victory. Total secrecy along with a diversionary move would be necessary.

The bit of rum and his nearly total recall of the victory at Stony Point brought a smile to Wayne's face, even as his foot and ankle continued to ache. The normal sounds of army camp activity were lost to him as he continued to recall the successful assault on the heights of the Stony Point fortifications. Ignoring a nagging sense of duties that needed attention, he re-lived the final hours of the victory.

Urging complete silence, the men were mustered and ordered to hold off the attack until after ten o'clock on the night of July fifteenth, 1779. Each man was instructed to attach a fragment of white cloth or paper to his hat. This was done to avoid confusion and possible injury to fellow soldiers during the dead of night. In order to prevent even an inadvertent musket shot, which would alert the British of the coming assault, General Wayne gave strict orders that no weapon should be loaded. The men's whispered remarks and curses proved the order to be an unsavory one. Wayne ignored them and gave the order to "fix bayonets".

A broad grin stretched the General's cheeks as he was finishing his revelry. The victory had been complete! The Americans had lost only twenty killed and eighty wounded. Over five hundred British prisoners were taken.

*   *   *

The General was not ashamed of the few minutes he had taken to re-live that memorable battle during the American Revolution, but now it was time to move the troops toward his next objective, the Indian village of Red Bird.

"General Wayne sir, begging your pardon but Major Scott says the troops are ready to march at your command."

"Any final details that need my immediate attention, Lieutenant?"

"Well sir there's the matter of that Indian scout as is called Tom. The one that deserted sir."

"I have no time for that now. Prepare for the order to march."

A private was repeatedly clearing his throat outside of Wayne's tent.

"See what that man wants, then get rid of him," Wayne ordered.

The man parted the tent flaps and stood at rigid attention. "There's a problem with some of the horses, General," he said, staring straight ahead.

"What sort of 'problem'?" Wayne growled.

"Well sir, the problem is that . . .well they said . . ."

"Speak up man! We are busy here. The problem?"

"Well sir them horses, well some of them anyway, about forty or so, just naturally got loose in the night and well they just naturally run off! Sorry to tell you sir."

"Dismissed," Wayne said. He turned to the waiting Lieutenant. "Time will be lost until the animals are rounded up. I want the names of the sentries who were posted around the corral last night."

"Sir, I'm sorry to tell you that both sentries are dead, Sir!"

"Indians?" Wayne asked, perturbed.

"I'm afraid so, sir. They musta took about a dozen mounts, then turned the rest loose. The men are after the strays now, General."

"What about the guards?"

"Dead and scalped, Sir."

Wearily, Wayne turned again to the matter at hand. "While we wait I will see the Indian scout accused of desertion. He is in stocks somewhere in the camp. By the way, find a private by the name of O'Casey, and a Private Caswell. Bring them to me. Dismissed."

"Stand up, you!" the Lieutenant snapped, yanking Tom to his feet. The Indian staggered a step or two, his legs numb again after yet another night in irons. He was hungry, thirsty, and very tired, but was shoved along by the lieutenant's rifle, which was pushed into his back. "Keep moving, redskin. The General is in a hurry this morning. Probably won't take more than a few minutes to arrange for your 'necktie party'!"

Sean and Big Cas were already near headquarters when Tom and his escort arrived. Sean tried to get close enough to his friend to speak to him, but Cas shoved him roughly away. "None of that, soldier!" Big Cas said. "You two ain't going to get a chance to get together and make up some more lies for the General. Keep him moving, Lieutenant!"

The Lieutenant gave him a withering look. "Keep your mouth shut, Cas," he said under his breath. They were at the tent's door flap now, but hadn't yet been given permission to enter.

Private Caswell, true to his nature, yelled out, “We’re here, General Wayne, Sir. Permission to enter?”

“Come in and be quick. There is much to be done. As soon as the missing horses are rounded up, we march!”

Tom stood before the General, head hanging. He had little hope for his chances for mercy. During the night he had berated himself for not breaking away when he’d had the chance. A bullet did not seem at all bad when compared to what was surely coming next!

General Wayne began the questioning without preamble. “Of what tribe are you, and who was your war chief?”

“I am Wyandot,” Tom said, still not making eye contact with his inquisitor. “My chief is . . .I mean was . . .Roundhead. His Indian name is Styathica ‘The Bark Carrier’. The one above him was Tarhe ‘The Crane’.”

“You are aware, are you not, that this man,” he indicated Big Cas, “is accusing you of being a spy for the British. This is in addition to the known fact that you twice attempted to desert from the army. What do you have to say for yourself?”

Tom was so hungry and thirsty that coupled with the life-endangering charges being leveled against him he felt that he might faint. “I will tell thee all that has gone on with me, but I need water to drink, lest I fall.”

“Don’t listen to him, General,” Cas stated. “He’s just trying to sound like Bible talk and lead you down the wrong trail with all that 'thee' stuff! If I was you . . ."

"You are not me Caswell! Do not speak further unless spoken to."

"Sure! Sure. I'll keep my old trap shut unless . . ." The General's scathing look finally silenced the big soldier.

"Now Tom Bluefoot, you can see how suspicious it looks that you suddenly join up to scout for us after all you claim has happened to you. Explain yourself, but be quick."

"I was sold by my Indian father because . . ."

"I am aware of that. You told it to me before. What happened when you returned to Little Turtle's village?"

"As thou wilt learn, I lived there for I think two winters. I and some other boys used to sneak up behind the lodges when big councils were happening. I learned much, especially since I spoke the white man's tongue. I heard things that the British said to our chiefs before their words were changed to ours by the translators."

"Yes, I heard some of this story before. Can you name any of the British officers that you heard?" Wayne asked, fixing his eyes on the scout.

"As I told you before, Alexander McKee was one, but I can't remember the names of any others, if I heard them."

"You sound almost believable Tom Bluefoot, but there is one major question that must be answered. Why did you leave your Indian father and your people to join an enemy army? I find this hard to swallow."

"A long story is necessary, but to save thee time I will only say that I had to leave," Tom mumbled, searching the General's face.

"Had to?" Wayne said. "And why was that?"

"Don't listen to him, General! Hang the lying varmint so we can get on the march. I told you before . . ." Cas began, but a look from General Wayne silenced him yet again.

"Thou can believe me or not, but I fled in the night after what my white father, Eli Miller, would call a murder! I killed, then I ran. I came here because I thought I might be able to hasten the end of the war that all of us, red man and white, know is coming."

"You would stop the coming war? And just how may I ask did you plan to do that?" Wayne was almost smiling at the ridiculous notion being put forth by the skinny, shivering Indian.

"I know Chief Blue Jacket's plans!"

Wayne stared at the scout in astonishment. "You expect me to believe such a story?" He exclaimed. "Just how did you manage to learn that information, and, if it is true, why would you choose to reveal it to the American army?"

"Eli Miller, the man who bought me from my real father, was a man of peace. He is of a tribe called 'Quakers'. They are all men who believe in keeping the peace. They are trusted by most of our tribes;

Wyandot, Shawnee, Miami, and so forth. That is where I learned about the white man's God. Eli said all wars are evil and that his God hated bloodshed and killing. But I could never understand . . ."

"Excuse me General," the Lieutenant said, sticking his head in between the door flaps, "but Scott ordered me to inform you that the horses are secured and we are ready to march. Your orders, Sir?'"

"Scott is in charge. Move the troops regiment by regiment in the usual order. I will be joining up shortly. Dismissed."

"You were saying there was something you could not understand. And what was that, Tom Bluefoot?"

"Yes General Wayne. I could not understand why your people always claimed that you wanted peace with your red brothers, but still you took our land, broke the treaties that you made, killed our women and children, and burned up our houses and our corn!"

"See what I mean, General," big Cas exclaimed. "I told you he was a liar!"

Now you can see for yourself what I been telling you all along. And another thing. I'll bet he was in on the theft of our horses last night. Probably signaled to his red brothers and told 'em how to go about taking them and killing our pickets."

"That would be a little difficult to accomplish don't you think, seeing as how this scout was in irons all the time that he wasn't here with me," Wayne answered him mildly. "I've made my decision. Have General Scott enter and observe as I pass sentence."

Tom felt as if his legs had turned to butter and would not much longer keep him from falling.

"You'll not be hanged for your crimes, Tom Bluefoot, but by the time your sentence is carried out you may wish you had! General Scott, please take written notes of the sentence and enter them into the log."

Wayne's Second-In-Command produced a small notebook and a lead pencil. "Ready when you are Sir," he said, seating himself on a folding camp chair. He balanced the booklet on his knee and waited expectantly.

"It is my studied opinion that you had justifiable provocation to run from an admitted Indian hater twice your size," he began. "Still you did desert, and having done so, must accept your punishment. Lieutenant," he called, "muster the remaining troops to observe a flogging."

Tom's heart sank. Some, he knew, after being punished in this way nearly died. It all depended upon the number of lashes ordered. He waited, standing at attention as best he could.

"Following discipline," Wayne continued hurriedly, "this man, Private Caswell, and Private O'Casey will proceed with extreme caution to the village of Little Turtle. The two white men are to remain in hiding nearby while the scout enters the camp of our enemies. He is to gather any pertinent information which may help our cause. The three will then return and report directly to me, not more than two weeks from today. I have no doubt," he continued ironically, "that Private Caswell will be more than happy to see that O'Casey and the scout return to our lines!"

"Excuse me, General, but I don't believe you specified the number of lashes for punishment."

"Indeed I did not. Tom Bluefoot is to receive three lashes 'well laid on', Private O'Casey one lash, and our champion marksman, none."

Shakily, tom spoke up. "Sir I deserve my punishment, but Private O'Casey did nothing wrong! Sir!"

"It has been reported that he brought food and water to a prisoner. The Punishment stands!"

"Uh . . . did you . . . I mean, sorry Sir but did you say 'three lashes' for Tom Bluefoot? Is that correct Sir? Only three?"

"Do you have a hearing problem? That is exactly what I said. Three for the Indian, and one for O'Casey. These three will be extremely fortunate if they even make it to the enemy camp without detection, let alone get back to our lines alive. Do you have every word of this down in the log?"

"Yes sir! Every word. I believe all remaining troops are assembled on the drill field. The flogging can begin at your command."

* * *

Little Turtle sat unmoving as the sweat trickled down his cheeks. The Council House was sweltering.

Not only were the door flaps closed, but the council fire, albeit a very small one, was adding to the heat. Blue Jacket of the Shawnees was talking. He had been doing so since the sun had set and the moon risen. This was his right and privilege. All sixty or more assembled there would agree on that point. Their turn would come as the two week long Council continued.

"They have burned two more of our villages. Furthermore you all know," at this point he turned slightly to his left and looked directly at Chief Little Turtle, "that in the last atrocity an old woman, unable to walk, was found and stabbed to death with the long knives the soldiers fasten to the ends of their rifles!" He paused for effect, still gazing at the other chief. "That woman, Sei-Chi-Watipa, was the sister of my grandmother!" While he did not raise his voice, the intensity of his gaze and the bitterness of the words he had used did not go unnoticed by a single person assembled there.

Little Turtle waited for a respectful moment or two then stood to his feet. At that moment a rustling sound could be heard from the northern bark wall. A young brave stood and headed toward the opening. There was no mystery about the sounds. Young boys, curious about proceedings within, and anxious to become warriors themselves, were pressed against the wall, listening. With a quick gesture the chief bade the man sit back down. A half smile lighted his face as he recalled many times when as a lad, he and his friends had done the same thing!

"Brothers," he began, swinging his eyes around and into the farthest recesses of the Council House, "I am not a stranger to anyone here. You know me, and I know you. You have had many opportunities to watch me in battle. Several of you have fought by my side. Some have fallen for the final time. Together, you and I, as well as many braves not present here on this night, won great victories against the whites. The soldiers of him who is called Har-a-Mar, as well as those of Saint Clair, fell in defeat!" There was a general, respectful murmuring of appreciation and agreement. "Who among you can stand and accuse me of cowardice?" Almost to a man the listeners vehemently denied any such thought. "And who can say to this war council that I did not lead us well?" Several were now shouting that they certainly had no such opinions about their chief.

"So it is neither lack of courage nor the inability to lead which brings me to suggest to all that while we are in such a position of strength we begin the process of negotiating for a favorable end to the wars with the white man." After sweeping his eyes once again to all present, he sat down.

Blue Jacket stood again. "Let all gathered here be assured that I have only the greatest respect for our principal chief, Little Turtle! I have nothing but the highest regard and respect for him as a warrior and as a wise and capable leader. Still I would ask why he feels that negotiations with the whites would be a good policy at this time. As he has already said, we have beaten them twice in recent battles. As it is told 'when the buffalo is wounded and tired, even the squaws can make a kill'. The Shawnees say 'stand and fight the Shemanese once and for all!'" A chorus of shouts and growls of agreement followed Blue Jacket's oration.

But Little Turtle was not yet finished. As before, he waited patiently until quiet resumed. Then once again he stood before them, a look of quiet resignation pulling his eyelids low. He knew that whatever argument he might make, and no matter how eloquent his speaking, they wanted war! And who could blame them? Many of their homes destroyed, carefully tended crops burned or deliberately trampled by Wayne's cavalry, sons and daughters shot down, their bodies left unburied. Still he knew he must try.

"Brothers," he began earnestly, "I know your hearts. I remember your many acts of bravery and cunning. You have made the hearts of my sons swell with pride. We have defeated a powerful enemy. Yes, we have defeated him twice!" There were a few triumphant shouts from the listeners. "But hear me this one more time, valiant ones. You are witnesses of the arrogant men often parading about our villages in their coats the color of fox blood. They pledge their help in our cause against the advancing army. That is good. They have guns which do not fall apart after but a few shots. The metal buttons on their coats shine like the eyes of the deer in bright moonlight. Yes, they look like the very greatest of warriors. But . . ." The chief paused for such a long time that some of those assembled shifted positions and cast questioning glances at their companions. Finally Little Turtle resumed his oration.

"Lately, in the night, I have begun to hear some bad birds speaking outside my wegiwa. 'About the British,' they seem to be saying, 'can they really be trusted to do all they have been promising in our behalf? If the coming battle should go badly for the red man, will they bring their great guns and their sabers to turn the tide in our favor?"

Breaking all protocol, Blue Jacket leaped to his feet and shouted, "You have all seen that the Redcoats have built a mighty fort not far to the north of our villages. Should the forces of him who is called 'Mad Anthony' by his own soldiers, appear to be winning, we will be able to enter that fort where even the Americans' cannon will be worthless! Again I say, the Shawnees seek war!" He sat down as shouts and war cries once again exploded within the Council House walls.

Still standing, Chief Little Turtle could hardly be heard as he announced, "You have spoken. We will fight."

*　　　　*　　　　*

Both Sean and Tom had been stripped to the waist and tied to trees a few paces apart. All troops not already on the march were arranged rank and file to witness the whipping. Wayne had no choice but to deal harshly with deserters, always the bane of any army made up of regulars and volunteers. Indeed over a dozen had been hanged during this campaign alone. In view of this, the watching soldiers were amazed at what was certainly the lightest such sentence they had ever seen!

The punishment had been placed in the hands of Major Arthur Benjamin. He signaled for a drum roll as a burly soldier stepped forward, pulling and stretching the "tails" of the ugly device. An exact replica of the instrument that had been used by sea captains for generations. Each of the leather strands was tipped with a bit of metal, meant to further cut and gouge the unfortunate victim.

Just as the punishment was about to begin, General Wayne suddenly motioned to the sergeant holding the whip. Heads together they conversed for a moment. Tom's hopes soared, then as quickly fell as the man with the whip returned. He set himself, drew back his arm and "well laid on" the first blow.

Tom would have screamed had he enough breath to do so. The lash had stretched across his left shoulder blade, then curled nearly all the way around his chest. Blood was already forming along the gashes and puncture wounds when the second blow fell. Tom did scream then. The third lash was doubly painful as the singing leather bit into the cuts and welts already striping his body. The scout did not faint, but had he not been securely tied he would certainly have fallen.

Despite being tied to the tree Sean stood at attention as best he could. Tom, eyes closed in pain could not see what next happened to his friend. It was well that he could not! The sergeant obeyed the whispered order General Wayne had given him at the last moment. The bloody cords whipped forward, slashing Sean high on his shoulders. Two of the strands cut across his neck and into his face. Bleeding gashes appeared instantly. One metal tip dug into the young Irishman's left eye! Sean hugged the sapling he was tied to, his body racked with silent sobs.

When each man had been released they simply lay in bloody heaps, only half conscious. The standing troops had laughed when Tom's punishment was meted out. Not so as the lash cut across their fellow soldier's face! It was obviously deliberate. To a man, the troops were incensed by this. Punishment was to be expected but not in the face! Those close enough had no doubt that Sean would never see out of that eye again. Something like a low growl began in the ranks, but before their outrage could be allowed to grow, the order to "quick march" was hastily given. They trotted off the drill field, hurrying to rejoin the comrades who had left before.

Two camp followers, Sarah and Eve, fell to their knees and began to clean Sean's wounds, the army surgeon having left by wagon an hour before. With little to work with they did the best they could. The ladies ignored Tom Bluefoot completely. Who would care what happened to him? He was only an Indian anyway!

Whether Sean was sobbing or not was impossible to tell. His whole body was shaking so hard his blood spattered the women's arms as well as the leaves and grasses nearby. After smearing the most serious cuts and gouges with grease, they bound nearly his whole head and face with strips of linen. These were soon soaked through.

Tom was in agony, but even so he felt a great compassion for the pain being experienced by his friend. After all, he told himself, Sean would not be suffering like he was, were it not for an attempt to help his Indian friend!

Tom lay on his stomach, feeling somewhat better as his back and sides were becoming slightly numb. Sean sat hunched over, both hands gently enfolding his bloody bandages. He moaned softly as his body continued to shake. The women soon left, hurrying away to follow the marching army.

Sean arose first, rearranging the bandages around his head in order to make a hole for his only good eye. Tom regained his feet as well, moving with extreme caution, hoping to keep the cuts from bleeding worse.

Big Cas ambled up, a cruel grin on his face. "Well ain't you-uns a sorry-looking pair?" he gloated. "I reckon we better go at a dog trot for the first half day or so! Haw haw."

Neither Sean nor Tom dignified his taunts with a reply. Holding on to each other they followed Caswell to his small tent, which had not yet been taken down. "You better not put your shirt on, Injun,"Cas laughed. "If you do you ain't never going to get it off when them cuts dries up. If I was you I'd try to stick some lard or something on your back. And you'd better do it pretty soon too!"

Tom suspected that Big Cas was right about that, but he didn't have any lard to use. He decided that he would just carry his buckskin shirt for a few days until his wounds started to heal.

Cas rounded up two army stragglers and made them strike the tent. They carried it off, heading north and cursing Cas under their breath as they went. Tom, Sean, and Cas did not follow them. Their route toward the hostiles' camps would avoid any part of the trail made by the advancing army. One of the many narrow, almost invisible Indian trails Tom Bluefoot knew of would provide their highway into extreme danger.

It would not be until some months later that Sean would be able to personally thank General Wayne for ordering the deliberate wound that had effectively saved him from a slow and cruel death at the stake by the Indians.

* * *

The fort called Greenville had gone up rapidly. Wayne's strict and unbending discipline had converted the mostly lazy, independent-thinking rabble into an army! Whether felling trees for fortifications, marching, or engaged in musketry practice, the men had learned to respond to orders smartly and without question. While the General was well aware that there were those among the ranks who secretly ridiculed his insistence upon managing his army in the same fashion as he had done so successfully against the British during the recent Revolution, he was not to be dissuaded.

"What's old 'spit-and-polish' need with all of these here forts for? A twenty year old volunteer griped, tossing another stick on the fire. "Why don't he just march us right up north to where everybody knows the Redskins is at? Why we could take keer of them varmints in a couple of days! But here we are, notching logs for loop holes to shoot out of. Well, says I, what's we supposed to shoot <u>at?</u> There ain't a Injun nor a Redcoat anywhere near where we are now." He pulled the kettle off the cooking fire, dug out a spoonful of cornmeal mush and blew on it a minute.

At eighteen years, the man's tent-mate tended to look up to his older companion. "You got that right, Brady, he agreed, Everbody knows Indians ain't about to stand and fight like real soldiers. Why if them devils sees an army coming at them they just runs and hides in the woods. Then they can shoot our ranks full of holes, us being all in a line and all together so they can't hardly miss, even if most of them can't shoot straighter than a dog's hind leg."

"A little late supper gentlemen?" The two soldiers leaped to their feet, knocking the stew kettle into the fire. They came to rigid attention, their faces white with fear. "Sorry to have startled you, but I was passing by and heard your remarks. Stand at ease." Neither recruit relaxed a single muscle. Both were thinking the same thing; "how many lashes for insubordination?"

"We're really sorry General Wayne, we surely are, but just a little soldierly griping sir. Meant no harm by our talk. None at all!" Brady stammered.

"Our supper is late because we had to do extra drills this evening. Hope you won't take it wrong, General. What we was saying I mean. We don't know nothing about how to fight a war, and I for one, surely knows that <u>you do!</u> See, I was with your army at the Stony Point battle."

"So you were there too, were you? If all the men who claim to have taken part in that campaign were here now, the army would be twice its size! And just how old are you, Private?"

"I'm twenty sir. I mean uh . . ." Brady faltered. He had made a bad blunder, but it was too late to do anything about it now.

"You must have been the youngest man in the army at that time. I calculate that would have made you just about thirteen years of age then! Correct?" He used one highly polished boot to nudge the cooking pot upright, a bit of smoking gruel remaining in it.

Still standing at attention, neither man could think of a single thing to say. They waited to hear what their punishment would be.

"There are others who feel as you do about the military strategy I intend to use against Little Turtle and his fellow chieftains. Most of those are of much higher rank than either you two, of course. Still I am not to be deterred. I have every intention of making sure that when the battle is joined, and a decisive victory won, it will signal the end of our nation's Indian problems for good! As you were gentlemen. Finish your supper. Good night."

The two men turned slowly and stared at each other in profound shock. They were still standing at attention for another five minutes! Their cornmeal mush was forgotten.

*　　　　*　　　　*

"Are you sure, General? Some of the non-coms are asking about the direction of our route."

"Quite sure, Major. I can understand their concern. I am setting direction for the site of St. Clair's defeat. This puts our route at slightly west of north. Still, we will be moving generally toward the British and savages' army."

"Are you then expecting another attack in that area, General?"

General Wayne gingerly lifted his aching, gout-ridden leg from the stirrup, wincing in pain. The inflammation was causing him agony once again. Both fellow officers and troops were secretly wondering if their commander would even be able to lead in the anticipated engagement, especially if he had to be mounted.

At length he replied. "An attack by Blue Jacket's army is certainly a possibility, but the primary purpose of our route is to bury the remains of those troops slaughtered and mutilated in the 1791 defeat. After completing this unsavory task we shall erect a new fort. This will provide another site for the repository of supplies and reserves in our march toward the hostiles."

The major did not reply at first. Their horses continued moving at a slow walk. Wayne could tell that his companion had serious doubts about the wisdom of another such diversion in their plans to engage the enemy. It was, after all, December of 1793. Winter was upon them, always a major deterrent to the movements of any army.

After a few more moments of silence, the Major voiced his concern by way of a question. “Have you had reliable reports concerning the state of the battle ground, Sir? Perhaps over-zealous scouts exaggerated conditions there.”

“That is possible of course, Major, but I have information from a variety of sources that I feel are reliable. According to these witnesses the bones and skulls of American army soldiers lie scattered over the ground for a distance of several acres. Most, if not all, show obvious signs of mutilation and torture.”

“As commander-In-Chief of our new American army I cannot in good conscience allow the remains of our gallant troops to lie in disarray, unburied.”

“Since you put it that way, I can but wholeheartedly agree. It will also be a boost in morale for our soldiers. Compassion for the fallen is a fine attribute for any in command, friend or enemy!”

“Thank you Major,” Wayne said, once again trying to find a less painful position for his throbbing foot.

Two days later the column arrived at the site of the worst disaster in the history of an American army. As had been reported, bones littered the ground in such profusion that it was necessary to brush them aside in order to find room for the troops to pitch their tents. Numerous burial details began work immediately and continued for three days until the grisly task was completed.

Six months later, construction of what Wayne named Fort

Recovery was completed under the direction of Major Burdeck and the infantry. In July of 1794, Blue Jacket's warriors, against the advice of several other chiefs and a few British officers, would attack the new fort. The former victory and slaughter of St. Claire's troops at this very site had given him much incentive to repeat this major event.

*   *   *

"Tell them the story," Blue Jacket's wife, Wabethe, "The Swan", repeated, poking her husband with one bare toe. It was hot in the lodge, but they liked the light from the tiny central fire. "Go ahead, it will help take your mind off the coming battle."

"I am not afraid!" Blue Jacket growled. "Besides, you have all heard the story of my days as a hated Shemanese. Why tell it again?"

"Tell it father! Tell it! We love to hear the story. We are not sleepy yet," his only son begged, leaning back against his mother.

After a long pause, the handsome young man did begin to speak. All present knew that long before he had finished his tale the children would be fast asleep.

"Blue Jacket sighed, composed himself and began. "I was a mighty warrior. Not only had I killed hundreds of buffalo, dozens of white bears, and two double hands of panthers, but . . ." Laughing, Wabethe pushed against her husband's arm. "No, my husband. The children are too old for such nonsense. It is time they heard the truth of your wise decision to leave the white man's world and become one of us. Be serious now. They should be told."

Blue Jacket took time to light his pipe, then began. This time his voice was serious and solemn. "My parents were good people, but they knew nothing of the proper way to raise a warrior son. When I did something wrong, which was quite often, my father, who is called Jeremiah Von Swearingen [one of the daughters laughed to hear such a ridiculous-sounding name] would hit me many times across my behind with part of a horse harness."

"Oh father, no!" the boy gasped. "He did this <u>on purpose?</u> No wonder you ran away to us. I would have done so had I been shamed in such a way. Did anyone <u>see</u> this disgrace?"

"All my brothers were <u>made</u> to watch. It was father's way of teaching them to avoid doing anything wrong. He told them that the same would happen to them if they did wrong. But that is not the real reason that I ran away."

"What <u>was</u> the real reason then?" Wabethe asked, her dark eyes shining in the firelight.

"It is simple. For all my childhood I wanted to become an Indian. One of the <u>real People!</u> I was lucky that an old man of the Miami tribe became my teacher. We spent many hours in the forests and along the streams near my home. This old person could no longer walk well, but he leaned on me and I helped him. He taught me more than just the skills of hunting and fishing. Much more!"

The children had fallen asleep as Blue Jacket and The Swan had known they would. Still he continued his narrative. Sometimes she would ask a question or two, speaking in her usual, soothing voice. "You have become a better warrior than any of those born in our tribe. Moreover, you are a most loving [and here she giggled a little] husband. Also, my Blue Jacket is the kind of father that you did not have in your youth. I am proud of my man!"

"I was not prepared for much of the adoption process of our people," Blue Jacket mused. "For one thing, like everyone, white and red alike, I had heard of the custom called 'running the gauntlet.' In my pride I had assumed that it was comprised of only a few women and children using small switches that might sting a little. After all had not my father done much worse with the piece of horse harness that he used? How wrong I was! Not only was there the use of real clubs by grown men and older boys, but the beatings were repeated in every village to which I was taken. I feared for my life, or worse, a crippling injury! You have never been told that in truth I failed the tests, fainting at the end of nearly each of the long lines. I had shown true courage however and I was forgiven. When I was sufficiently recovered I was dragged into the river. Two squaws stripped me of every garment and used river sand to scrub me all over. This, they said was to wash away everything white from my body. I think," he said as she giggled "you would have liked to be in on that!"

"There is much, much more I wish to tell you but now I am tired. I must sleep, for the assault on the white men's fort will begin at dawn.

* * *

"Pine sap might help these cuts heal," Tom suggested, rinsing Sean's bandages in the creek. "The old woman who raised me while Pa was drunk had a whole parfleche full of plants she gathered in the woods. She used pine sap a lot on cuts."

Sean flinched as Tom retied the linen strips around his head. "Easy Tom! Easy!" he groaned as the wet strips tightened. "Tom, tell me the truth. How does my eye look?"

"I'll tell you how it looks, Red. It looks like hell! You'll be lucky if it don't get infected!" Caswell snorted.

Cas had taken charge of their journey. "I don't see as there's any hurry on this march," he had said two days before. "With all them cuts you two won't be able to march more than forty miles a day anyway! Ha ha"

Tom and Sean had tried to doctor each other's wounds, but had had little success. Cas was no help at all of course, but he had brought down a doe with his prized rifle. "You better enjoy this here venison, cause once we get closer to Injun country I ain't doin' any shootin' less I spot a Injun or two! Alright Stink Foot, you Indians is supposed to know all the trails in this here country. What's the best way north? We better get started tomorrow."

Tom could never trust the big soldier, so he was cautious about his answers. Still he told him what the best way would be.

"How do you know all this stuff?" Cas growled. "You're nothing but a Spy!"

"I'm not a spy for my people, but I intend to be the best one I can be for the Americans! That is if they let me back into Little Turtle's village and I can get out again. Does that answer thee?"

With an oath, Cas kicked him in the side. "Don't you use that church talk on me! There could be a accident somewhere in these woods and you two shirkers would never be found! So mind your tongue! You too, O'Casey!"

"Take it easy, Cas. That's just the way Tom learned English. He's ahead of us. He can talk two languages, us only one! Tom, if you're hurting as bad as I am why don't you tell us about what the Quakers believe. Maybe it'll take our minds off the pain for a while."

Cas suddenly lumbered to his feet and plodded off into the forest. Tom and Sean looked at each other in surprise. Who knew what the big soldier was up to? Sean scooted around until he could reach his musket. "You ain't aiming to shoot him are you?"

"We ain't either one of us going to shoot him, much as he deserves it. I still intend to see our mission accomplished. I got a whipping I didn't deserve, and I'm probably going to lose my eye on account of it, but I'm still a soldier. A soldier does his duty!"

Shortly Cas emerged, rifle on his shoulder. "I got mighty tired of hearing your complaints about a few little scratches, so I brung you some pine sap. Good luck smearing that on your cuts. I can't hardly get it offn my knife, so it'll probably feel real good when you start rubbing that in! Haw haw!"

"It'll have to be softened up some way," Tom said. "The old Kickapoo woman I stayed with boiled them in a copper kettle."

"Thanks Caswell," Sean said. He was unable to see the man's expression in the flickering firelight. Big Cas did not respond.

"Well Injun, you gonna tell us all about them cowards that raised you? The ones kept saying 'thee' and 'thou' all the time?"

Tom was too busy trying to scrape some of the resin off the bark, but it was too sticky. "Gimme that!" Cas said disgustedly. He grabbed the bark, broke it into pieces, and popped the fragments directly into the boiling water, sap and all.

"Now let's hear about them crazy people."

"I don't remember much about it. I was pretty small when Eli bought me. Mostly they called themselves 'Friends'. They said all wars were wrong and everybody should just get along. He made me go to his 'Meeting House' once a week. I never could quite figure out what was going on in there. Much of the time nobody said anything!"

"So if a Injun, or say a robber, was to come in his house to kill him, he wouldn't shoot first?"

"I guess he wouldn't, but we had some Delawares come once. He gave them food and they just slept on the floor all night."

There was no response from Caswell. Soon they heard him snoring.

*   *   *

"Half day ahead," the scout reported, drinking scalding hot tea laced with sugar. "Four double hands lodges, and one hand lodge more. Not many warriors. Much corn, squash. I sleep now." He stalked away, tired from an all-night vigil near Many Trees' village.

"What did he say, George? I can't follow their lingo. Has the Major given the order yet? Some hare-brained hot head's liable to start the fight before we get up there!"

"Best I can tell the scout said about forty lodges. They call them 'wegiwas'. I don't trust some of them scouts, especially the Miamis. Most of the men from the village are probably further north, to join up with Little Turtle and Blue Jacket. They know we're coming, but don't know when. Come to think of it, I don't know when either!"

Just after dawn Major Burdeck led the troops up an Indian trail which followed the Auglaize. The infantry led, with the cavalry following. Complete silence had been ordered, but everyone knew that in a moving army silence was nearly impossible. The sun was still not above the trees when the small village came into view. The site had been well chosen. The Major and two lieutenants had moved to the head of the column and were silently observing the scene. Wisps of smoke curled upward from a few cooking fires, but strangely enough no squaws could be seen tending them. "I don't like it Major," one of them said. "It looks mighty peaceful. They had to know we were coming. They always have sentries out, just like we do. Better be careful!"

"Nonsense, Martin. You can see cooking fires. I counted eleven horses tethered just north of the village. The savages love their horses. If they were expecting an attack they would have hidden them in those woods yonder. We are undetected. Give the order!"

Two years of unrelenting discipline was evident as the men made an orderly advance. A very old woman crossed the creek and stood silently, making no effort to flee. The boom of a heavy charge from one of the new rifles echoed against the forest. She crumpled into the dirt. Two braves dashed from their lodges and leveled their muskets at the approaching army. One fired too soon. The other's gun misfired and he fell backward, shot through the head.

Suddenly war whoops erupted from the hickory grove to the north. Thirty mounted warriors came charging at the Americans. They released a volley that killed two men and wounded a sergeant's mount. Their other shots went wide.

The order, "Fire at will" was given. The soldiers dashed into the village, shooting down anyone who appeared. Mothers ran from their lodges, snatched up children, and ran for the trees. They were shot, some children killed by the same bullet that tore through their mothers. A few made the safety of the hickory grove and were pulled onto the backs of the horses.

The remaining Indians wheeled their mounts and disappeared. A few more shots were fired as the soldiers raced directly into the village. Abandoned and bewildered children were shot or bayoneted to death where they stood or ran. Then the looting and burning began.

There being no more resistance and nothing of much value to steal, they began to fire the wegiwas. The ascending smoke, seen for mile, served as dire warning to those watching to the north.

The cavalry galloped into the standing corn, the infantry following and picking up some of the undamaged ears. The corn was "in the milk" and would make fine roasting ears. Although the bean crop had already been harvested, and stored in large clay jars, most of it was also destroyed in the fires.

When the natives had made certain that Wayne's army had gone on to wreak havoc in other villages, the squaws and even a few braves returned to salvage anything that still remained. There was almost nothing. The coming winter would be a hungry one!

*   *   *

"You better get that there bandage offn his back, O'Casey. Looks to me like it's pretty well stuck on there. Should be real fun when it comes loose!" Big Cas chortled. "Here, let me do it for you. Better bite down on a stick or something Stink Foot. This ain't going to be pleasant!" Tom steeled himself and waited.

The bandages that Sean had made by tearing up a piece of his shirt were indeed bonded onto to the scout's cuts and abrasions. Tom could only wonder at how those who had received fifty or even a hundred lashes could have lived. Some hadn't! Soaking the cloth in the pine sap elixir didn't seem to help much. In fact it had made the bandages stick even tighter.

"Gimme the loose end of that bandage," Cas grinned. "Get ready Injun! This ain't gonna feel good!" He pushed the Indian to his knees and jammed one big boot across Tom's lower back. "You ready?" he asked sweetly, as Tom sweated in anticipation. "Are you sure you're ready for this 'cause it's gonna hurt like the very devil! But I'll just hold on for a while until you think you can stand it if . . ."

"Cut it out, Caswell," Sean said. "You've had your fun. Get it over with!"

"Hurry up, Cas, pull it off," Tom moaned.

"Well if that's what you want, here goes!"

The big private gave the cloth a sudden violent jerk. A rasping sound was followed by Tom's ragged breath. He did not cry out. Fresh blood oozed from several of the deepest gashes. "There, Stink Foot. I done you a favor. You can thank me for it as soon as you quit bleeding all over my boots! Haw haw."

Their fifth day was going better. Tom's wounds were healing nicely, but Sean was not so lucky. A milky film now covered his injured eye. He tired easily, and had not Cas constantly berated him, they would have made very little progress. "Told you!" Caswell gloated. "You got yourself a fever. You'll be lucky if it don't kill you before Little Turtle's warriors does it for you!"

Tom spoke up. "That's enough, Cas. It looks like his eye is gone. He don't need more mean talk from you. We'll be in real danger from now on. We'll have to work together now, or we'll all lose our scalps!" With that he slipped into the brush to relieve himself.

As if by design, the path was suddenly blocked by four Miami warriors, painted for battle. "Ah!" the leader hissed, " two easy scalps. I claim the one with the bad eye. I'll give his scalp to my woman. She likes red things!"

Tom burst out of the forest. "Ho, my brothers! Do not kill these two. They are mine! I'm taking the big one to my friend, Chief Pecksinikwa, Blue Jacket. He will reward me greatly. A Shemanese this big will take a long time to die.

He will provide much sport!"

"The red-headed one is deserting the army of the one they call 'mad', as am I. He and I have much information about the enemy that will be of great interest to our chiefs. Let us pass immediately!"

Sean and Cas had not said a word. They were astonished at the way Bluefoot was taking charge of the situation. Coming back from doing his business out of sight, he had snatched up Caswell's rifle, which was lying behind the log Cas was sitting on. "What's going on?" the soldier quavered. "What you been sayin' to them Varmints?"

"Keep your mouth shut, you fool!" Tom snarled.

The first warrior spoke up suspiciously. "You are of our people. How is it that you speak the white mans' tongue?"

Tom drew himself up importantly. "I will answer you in good time, but first I will ask you to tie this man's hands for me. I have been unable while holding my rifle."

"If the red-headed one is joining us as an ally why did you not have him hold the gun while you tied your captive's hands?" The other braves grunted and nodded knowingly at each other. The leader stepped forward, reaching for the rifle.

"You are most wise, friend," Tom said calmly, while keeping a tight grip on the weapon. "but you can see this man is sick. Sometimes he falls in a faint. He could not be trusted to guard this dangerous soldier."

Sean and the private looked blankly from one to the other, having no idea what was being said or what was going on.

A brave stepped forward, not convinced. "Why is it that you were off in the forest, leaving your prisoner unguarded?" The others nodded angrily.

Tom was secretly amazed at his own audacity and quick thinking. "I was testing the Shemanese," he boasted. "I was watching from cover. Had he tried to run I would have shot him in the leg. Of course I would not kill him. As I said, he is my prize for the amusement of our people."

For a moment the braves appeared satisfied. Once more, Bear, the leader, stepped forward. "That is a fine gun. Did you steal it? I will take it for my own."

"Of course I stole it! Do you think the soldiers would have just handed it to me? You cannot take it. It is a gift I promised to get for Chief Blue Jacket. As you know he was once a white man. Since I was raised by a cruel white master, my friend Blue Jacket and I speak the Shemanes tongue." Sweat was running down Tom's face, and he fought to hide his trembling. "He would surely take it back from you anyway, and he would not be happy about the loss of his gift!"

The Familiar mention of their chiefs had obviously impressed them, but they still were not quite convinced. "You claim to know our great chiefs quite well. We do not wish to doubt you but perhaps you could describe for us Chief Little Turtle's dwelling." The lesser warriors grinned knowingly.

Drawing himself up once again, Tom described the chief's wegiwa in great detail, then went on to enumerate the medals and bracelets the Miami chief customarily wore.

"Oha!" the leader said. "We can tell that you speak truth. We will accompany you to our village. We will arrive in triumph!"

"Please do not do this," Tom intoned. "As you can see, I am young and inexperienced. You are warriors, certainly having counted many coups. I have none. I wish to bring this deserter and the prisoner into our village by myself. If you also come, many would believe that it was you great warriors who captured the prisoner. Pardon my pride, but I wish this honor for myself."

"Of course! May Gitchie Mnitou protect you." They slipped silently away.

* * *

"All right, Stink Foot. You've had your fun. Now get these thongs offn my wrists. Them varmints got them so tight they cut off the blood!"

"Shut your mouth!" Tom screamed, landing a vicious kick on Caswell's shin. "Thou art an ignorant ox with half the brains of a flea." He continued to shout at the top of his lungs, towering over the soldier in rage. Cas stared at him in amazed consternation, too shocked to be enraged.

"What in hell you yelling like that for? You want to wake up every Injun for miles around here? You better get this rawhide off me right now or I'll kick the life right out of you!" He raged. "Sean, you get up and get me loose. You ain't that sick!"

Tom backed up a pace or two, pointed the rifle at Big Cas' chest, and cocked the hammer. "I intend to kill thee right now," Tom hissed, bringing the gun to his shoulder.

"Watch out!" Cas screamed. "That there gun's got a hair trigger! It could go off sure. I didn't mean anything by them names I called you. Just having a little fun. Now you put that hammer back down before I get shot!"

Suddenly Tom turned to Sean. "Get thee not up, Sean!" he roared. "Stay thee right down. Pretend like thee art about to vomit. Cas, get thee down on your knees like thou art begging me. Do it now!" He was becoming hoarse from all the shouting, but kept the rifle aimed at the big soldier's middle.

No one had seen him. None had heard him, but suddenly there he was, standing arms folded, surveying the scene. It was the big Miami; Bear!

"Oho, my brother, the great warrior. Thou hast returned. Wilt thou humble thyself to eat with me? There is plenty for two. That one [he pointed to Sean] is too sick to eat, and he [he spit in Caswell's direction] will remain hungry until he himself becomes food. Food for the ravens!"

Bear, who had been eyeing everything in the camp, then spoke respectfully. "I have no time to eat, for I must catch up with my companions who are already far down the trail. But I thank you. Another time you and I will dine together. Although you are young and inexperienced, there is much about you that is commendable. Here." He threw a coil of braided rawhide at Tom's feet. "I have advice for my young warrior friend. I came back to give you this rope. I will hold your rifle on your captive while you tie his ankles, one to the other like a hobbled horse. That will keep you safe until you are back among your people. The big white man will have to hop all the way!"

"Thou art most thoughtful my friend," Tom said, "but I am

unskilled in the kind of knots that will not become loose on the journey. I will hold the rifle if thou wilt be so kind as to secure the rawhide."

Bear smiled a little. "Young and inexperienced he may be," he thought, "but this lad is not a fool!"

"For the love of God, man, if you're gonna shoot me, get on with it! You dirty Redskin, I know what you're up to. You're gonna march me into them Injun villages and let them put me to the stake! Well, I'll get loose yet, and then we'll see how a red-hot gun barrel feels stuck in your ear!"

"Shut up I tell thee," Tom snarled. "All will be made clear if thou just keep on pretending to be begging for your life."

"Finished," Bear said, getting to his feet.

"My thanks, you big, fat, ugly, tub of lard," Tom said in English. Smiling sweetly, he continued. "May ants and porcupines infest you lodge. You are a coward and a complete fool! Go in peace."

The Miami gave one more careful look around, then hurried away down the trail.

"Tom," Sean hissed, "are you crazy? He'll kill us all!"

"He would if he spoke English. I insulted him to see if he understood our language. If so, I would have killed him and we would have had to make a run for it. But he didn't!"

Big Cas was staring at Tom, his mouth gaping open like a beached trout. "What happened?" he queried. "Let the hammer down on that piece! Point it the other way while you do it!"

"I think you just saved our bacon!" Sean exulted. "How did you know that one of them would come back?"

"I didn't know for sure, but the big one never looked like he believed our story. Black Pipe told me once that when in danger, always try to put yourself in your enemy's moccasins. So I did. I just asked myself what I would do If I were those Indians. The answer was that I'd just get out of sight and see what happened when we thought we were safe. It worked. We were lucky!"

"Bluefoot, at first I thought you had gone completely crazy, but then when you called that big Injun all them names I was <u>sure</u> of it!" [All were well aware that Big Cas had not called the scout "Stink Foot" this time!] "But why'd you keep using all them Quaker words for?"

"I didn't <u>think</u> he knew the white man's tongue, but if he did those words might have confused him a little."

"Enough of this palaver. Get these blasted bindings offn my hands, and my legs too. <u>Hurry up!"</u>

"Sorry Cas. Not yet. No, you're going to hop, hop, hop, right on down the trail for a ways. Then we'll move off the path and take cover. We'll watch our back trail for a while. If no one is following we'll untie you and give you back your gun. You'll be on your own then. Stay hidden. Don't fire the rifle unless you have no choice."

Tom scratched a rough map in the dirt. He pointed out the place where two small creeks merged before they joined with the Maumee. "I'll try to be there at moonrise three days from today. If Sean or I don't come, head back down the river and wait for the army to come."

They headed north, Sean, still sick, stumbling forward in the lead, Cas hopping along next, and Tom Bluefoot, rifle in hand, came last.

A few drops of rain began to make soft tapping sounds on the maple leaves above them. "Might as well get some sleep," Caswell said, yawning. "You never know when you won't be allowed any. Every soldier worth his salt can sleep any time and any place. Youuns ought to remember that!"

"Wish I could sleep," Sean groaned. "My eye hurts terrible. It just thumps every time my heart beats. I'm scared, Tom. What if my eye never heals? I'll be half blind!"

Tom had no answer. He got up and examined their surroundings. "Look at this," he said, pointing to a windfall nearby. Two tree trunks lay jammed together, one across the other. Beneath them was a sliver of dry ground, thick with fallen leaves. "If it starts raining harder we could crawl under there. Might keep the rain off."

"You lily-livers! A little rain ain't never hurt nobody. Might even get the smell offn you, Stink Foot!" Caswell had started it up again.

"Cut it out, Cas. Tom's done you no harm. Like he said, if we get out of this alive it will only be by getting along and helping each other. So quit the name-calling."

"Maybe if we tell something about each other it will help take your mind off the pain," Tom said. "How about it, Sean?"

Cas suddenly stood up. "Stink foot here can start by telling us what happened to make him run from the Injuns and join up as a scout for the army. I don't mind tellin' you two I never did trust him. Maybe he's a spy like some has been sayin'." Cas had soon forgotten how only the scout's quick thinking had undoubtedly saved their lives.

Tom kicked some leaves further beneath the logs and squeezed under. "We can all fit under here if the rain starts coming down harder. Sean, why don't thee tell about where thou grew up?"

Sean pulled his shirt partly over his head. "I don't think I better lie down. Whenever I do I get sick to my stomach. You talk, Tom."

"Yeah, you talk, Injun. Probably be all lies anyway, but maybe it'll be better than sittin' here like lumps. Go on, tell your story."

The rain held off. As Tom began speaking, the past came roaring back as if it were yesterday. He was not merely telling what happened, he was re-living it!

* * *

"The seven braves plodded into Little Turtle's village unannounced," Tom began. "Faces blackened, they were riding double on two horses. Three were walking, leading another two mares.

On each horse two bodies were tied, face down.

The wailing and screaming began immediately. Tom Bluefoot ran from his aunt's wegiwa and joined the impromptu procession moving toward the center of the town. A woman ran madly toward the horses and threw herself against the bodies, patting and stroking them. Word had preceded the braves' return and she had already been in mourning for a day and a half. Her husband, nephew, and two grown sons had been slain in a raid gone terribly wrong.

It was only then that Tom and some others noticed another walker. A little girl, ragged and dirty, was being jerked along by one of the Indians, her hands tied to a rope. She was thin and haggard-looking. Her brown hair had once been done in two braids which were full of burrs and tangles. Never had Tom seen such terror on the face of a child. When all had stopped, the girl dropped to the ground, crying soundlessly. She was barefoot, her legs and feet bleeding from many cuts and scratches.

"Aiiwee!" the fallen braves' mother screamed. She rushed upon the girl and began slapping and kicking her. Yanking the child erect by the rope, she began to rant and rave. So distressed was the widow that her hateful words could hardly be understood. One thing was plain to all however. "Tri-si-li-net!," she screamed over and over. "Revenge! Revenge!" She threw the child to the dirt and ran off, tearing her hair.

The little girl curled up in the dust, legs drawn up, and arms around her knees. She made a very small bundle! No one offered her help or solace. There was no doubt that the mother of the dead had claimed the little one. It would be the grieving woman's right to direct the torture and eventual death of the Shemanese child. This, as an attempt to pay for the loss of her loved ones.

Tom did feel a little sorry for the victim. His years with the Quaker, Eli, had changed some of his thinking, but not much. He was still an Indian!

The white girl was dragged off to a fallen down hut at the edge of the village. She was not tied, as it was obvious to all that she was too terrified to even think of escape. Also, where would she go? The nearest white settlements were hundreds of miles away. Bonds were certainly unnecessary!

Two days passed. The entire village was intent upon mourning the dead. The burial ceremony was held in a walnut grove near the river. The widow could be seen there often, prostrating herself, first upon one grave mound, then another. No one spoke to her. Of course no one said the names of the dead warriors. During the night the woman's screams of grief could be plainly heard throughout the village.

It was the third day after the tragic arrival of the raiding party. Tom Bluefoot had set off to gather sticks for his aunt's cooking fire. As he passed the shack where the white captive was held, he heard a soft whimpering sound coming from within. Curious, he peeked through a crack. The white child was curled in a corner, crying softly. An old man, Slab Rider, apparently her guard, was sitting across from the girl. He appeared to be almost asleep. As Tom loudly cleared his throat the man jerked awake and peered around, blinking. "Who is out there?" he asked, getting slowly to his feet.

"It is I, Toom-shi-Chi-Kwa. May I enter?"

"Of course. Perhaps you could keep watch over the Shemanese for me while I get my supper. You will find it boring duty. She will not eat, or even make signs. I will come back after I've eaten. Would it be too hard for you if I took a little nap after I eat?"

"I will watch her for a while, but not too long. I have a bundle of sticks for my aunt's cooking fire."

The old man waddled out, showing surprising speed. He was hungry!

Tom entered the hut, stood inside the door opening and gazed at the small bundle that was the captive. She cowered back, scrabbling until she was pressed against the bark wall. Her eyes were wide, and she moaned in terror at still another Indian coming to hurt her. Tom's heart went out to her in spite of himself. He knelt on one knee to better see her face. Her small mouth opened wide in what appeared to be a silent scream.

"Do not be afraid little one," he said gently. "I will not harm thee." Slowly she lowered her arms, with which she had covered her face.

"Are you . . . are you a angel?" she whispered through bruised and cracked lips.

"No," Tom answered with a smile. "I am not an angel. Why would thee ask that of me?"

"You look like a . . . a . . . Indian man but you talk like the . . . the Preacher man at the camp meeting." Her eyes were beginning to show a glimmer of hope.

"My name is Tom, little girl. I am an Indian but I lived with a white man for six years. He taught me the language you speak. Are you in pain?"

"I hurt all over! Oh I wish Momma was here!" At the mention of her parent she began to sob so hard her whole small body was shaking. "They're all dead!" she wailed. "Oh . . . OHhhh!"

"Do you wish to tell me what happened?"

Her words came pouring forth in a flood. No one had spoken to her for days. "It was almost night when we heard turkeys gobbling in the woods. Will, he's my bro . . . broth . . ." She broke down then and covered her dirty face with her hands. "I mean he was my brother before he run off in the woods. I think they kilt him dead!" She cried some more and got a case of hiccups.

"If it is too hard to think about, thee does not have to tell me."

If the pitiful creature heard him she gave no indication of it. Haltingly she continued. "Will said for Poppa to give him the gun and he'd get us a turkey for supper. He runned out, but what we heard wasn't no turkeys at all. It was . . . it was . . . Indians making gobble sounds in the woods. Momma hadn't barred the door, since she was waiting on Will to come back in. The Indians busted in on us! Oh Tom, they just pulled my Momma outside. She was screaming! Poppa tried to fight them, but they drug him out by the hog lot and hit him a whole lot of times with . . . with a big hatchet-like thing that had blood all over it! Oh Tom . . . Oh I can't stand it!" Once more she curled up, sobbing.

Tom Bluefoot's heart was broken. This small Shemanese had done nothing to deserve such horror. Worse, she had had to witness the whole thing. Awkwardly he sat down by her side and gathered her up in his arms. Her tears soaked his shirt. She did not wrap her little arms around him. In fact she hardly seemed aware of what was happening.

Almost too low to hear, she began again. "They was awful! I didn't know what had happened to my little brother. He's four years old. I took keer of him lots of times. He said I was his 'little mommy'." Tom felt his own eyes fill with tears as her story continued.

"Art thou hungry? Thirsty? Hast thou had any supper?"

"They throwed a little piece of meat in the dirt today. I can't eat nothing. That old man give me some water in a gourd but it was all dirty. I didn't drink none. We had a good dog. We called him 'Old Runner'. He tried to bite the Indians but they shot arrows in his neck and kilt him as soon as they came. They drug me away with them. When we got almost to the spring I seen they'd set our cabin on fire. They burnt it all up, but first they took our kettle and some of our clothes and things. Anything they wanted! They went to sleep then, but I couldn't. The next day one of the meanest ones of them showed me a rolled-up skin. As soon as I saw it I knowed it was off of Old Runner. Then he kept holding up some meat and acting like he was eating! Oh

Tom, they kilt our good dog, and then they et him!"

"Thou should rest now. It will do thee good to have told. Tomorrow will be a better day. I will come to visit if thee wants me to."

"Oh do come, Tom. Please do! You are my only friend and I'm afraid. Real afraid, Tom. All of them are so mean! Why do they hate me so, especially that one old woman? She comes here and yells at me. Sometimes she hits me or scratches me. Can you tell her I didn't do anything to anyone? Can you Tom?"

"I'll tell her," Tom said. "Now I must take firewood to my aunt. You go to sleep. Tomorrow will be better."

"Oh don't go yet, Tom, please. I'll tell you something if you don't go."

"The old man will be back soon, so tell me, but hurry."

"I have been praying to Jesus to kill me. Is that a wicked thing? I can't stand that all my family is kilt by Indians, even my dog! I think maybe Jesus can see how terrible it is for me. I know I'll go to heaven if I'm dead."

"That is good. My white man father told me all about your God and His Son. I don't think your God is angry that you prayed to die. You are a good little girl and you've done nothing wrong."

A halting step outside heralded the approach of the guard. Tom's mind was whirling, but he knew what he must do. "You are back, I see,"

Tom said as the old man tottered inside. “You look tired. How would you like it if I took your place guarding the white child tonight? You need your rest. Any fool can see that the Shemanese needs little guarding! I will see to it if you wish.” The guard’s wrinkled face lit up with pleasure.

“That is very kind of you, Toom-She-chi-Kwa,” he cackled. “Thank you!”

“You can do a small favor for me then. Take my bundle of sticks to the wegiwa of my aunt. You know where she lives, I think. Don’t tell her what I’m doing to help you. She wouldn’t approve. Tell her I will be night-fishing on the river.”

Mumbling happily the old man gathered up the sticks and ambled away.

Tom sat by the child, listening to her breathing. She was not asleep. He was angry at himself. “Why did I even come in here?” he thought. “There is nothing I can do for her.” He had seen the torture pole being set up in the center of the village. The horrible spectacle would probably begin at noon tomorrow. Every conceivable means of causing pain would be thrust upon her. The shrieks and screams of a Shemanese would only excite them more. A day, perhaps even two, the horror would continue, to stop only with her death.

The girl was making no sound, but Tom could see tears making clean streaks down her cheeks.

"Thou must sleep," Tom urged. He'd continued using the Quaker method of speaking, as it seemed to sooth her somewhat.

"Oh I don't want to go to sleep! Cause when I wake up you'll be gone and them mean Indians will hurt me again. Then I'll have to remember about Momma, Poppa, my little brother, and . . . and . . . Old Runner, and maybe even my big brother, Will. Oh Tom, talk to me some more, please!" She grabbed his hand and held on.

Tom Bluefoot squeezed her small palm. All sorts of desperate schemes crowded his brain. Could he take her and run for the river? That was nonsense. The white child could barely walk, let alone run. Perhaps he could carry her and make an escape. She certainly didn't weigh much. Escape to where? They would be caught before they'd gone a mile. Then Little Turtle's village would need a second torture pole. That one for him!

"Why ain't you saying nothing, Tom? Please talk. It helps me when you talk."

"All right," Tom said gently. "Do you know anything about heaven?"

"Oh yes I do. I'm going there some day."

Tom was truly amazed by that remark. "How dost thee know that thou will? Is that part of the white man's religion?"

For the first time the little girl began to relax a little. "Cause one time last fall the Braxtons brung a wagon, we didn't have one, and took us and them to what they called a 'camp meeting'. It was in the woods a long ways from our place. A big preacher-man told us all about heaven. Well me and Poppa kneeled down on a log, and we got Jesus in our hearts! Momma already had that, she said. I don't know about Will. He didn't kneel or nothing. I got Jesus in my heart Tom. Do you?"

Tom hesitated. "I think maybe I do. My white father talked about that a lot. He took me to his church house, but I couldn't really tell what was going on in there. He taught me a 'God Prayer'. He called it 'Now I Lay Me'. He made me say it every night before I went to sleep. I think I can still remember it."

"Oh Tom, I know that too! Could we say it now? Oh could we Tom?"

She pressed her head against his arm and waited expectantly. "If I get it wrong, thou will have to help me," Tom said. Their voices blended softly as they began:

Now I lay me down to sleep.

I pray the Lord my soul to keep.

If I should die before I wake,

I pray the Lord my soul to take.

"Now," Toom-She-chi- Kwa whispered, "thou must sleep, for tomorrow will be a much better day!" He helped her stretch out on the dirt floor and smoothed several strands of hair from her face. Totally exhausted, the little captive was asleep in minutes.

Tom looked up at a crack in the hut's roof. "White man's God," he whispered, "forgive me!" Careful not to wake her, he picked up a piece of old doeskin and folded it into a pad. Very quickly he pressed it hard over her face. When she began to thrash and struggle he leaned down hard with both arms. It was soon over. When he was sure, he arranged her arms by her side, brushed the hair back from her face once again, and straightened her legs. He studied her face. On it was a beautiful look of peace. "If there really are angels in the white man's religion, I reckon that's what one would look like," he thought.

He slipped silently out of the hut. Tom knew he must not run, as people would notice. But he did run! He couldn't help it!

He'd almost reached the river when a young brave shouted at him. "What are you running from Toom-She-chi-Kwa?"

Making no reply, Tom plunged in and let the current take him north.

It was raining harder then. Tom's story had taken longer than he could believe. Sean was asleep, or perhaps in a faint. Big Cas however was very much awake!

"That there girl you smothered to death," he began suspiciously, "did she have a front tooth missing?"

"I don't know if she did or not," Tom said. "I never seen it if she did. Why do you ask that?"

* * *

"Oha! A fine present! My wives will be happy, so then I will be happy as well!" Little Turtle fingered the bolt of blue and white muslin until the interpreter had fumbled his way through his words. He then continued. "Yes it is a very fine present, Colonel Alexander McKee. Surely this cloth must have been brought all the way from Detroit. Is that not correct?" This time the interpreter, a French voyageur who had lived with the Seneca, had even more trouble finding the proper British words. Little Turtle had all he could do to hide his impatience

At every council this same problem occurred. Every minor chief and war leader must have his say, then the words translated for any British officers present. Next of course would be the Redcoats' response and their words translated into the Indians' tongue! Patience was a virtue practiced by most Indians, but the process was indeed a tedious one. Accomplishing any sort of planning was next to impossible.

McKee, newly promoted to Colonel, spoke at some length. Heat in the council lodge was stifling, but of course no one considered leaving. Those British officers accompanying McKee perspired profusely in their tightly buttoned tunics, but they endured the discomfort. "The great King across the eastern sea sends his best wishes to his red brothers here in the wilderness of America," McKee continued. "He desires that all be good children who will fight against the palefaces who even now are marching toward your homes and villages. In order to show his good will to you, his allies in this land, your British 'Grandfather' has sent gifts, tokens of his love and esteem for the great chiefs and warriors who are gathered here this night!"

At a gesture from the new Colonel, a British officer stepped forward and handed him a small, highly polished mahogany chest, bound with brass. McKee handled it reverently but did not yet undo the clasp. He waited calmly as the inept interpreter struggled mightily with Colonel McKee's oration.

The Indians remained outwardly impassive, but the eyes of some, especially the younger among them, were shining in anticipation. Unsure if any were even able to grasp the meaning of his words, nevertheless with a dramatic flourish McKee opened the cask. It was filled with medals, brooches, and other such trinkets. While shiny and impressive looking to the natives, the cheap brass and nickel silver of which they were made would soon tarnish and the ribbons fade.

A British officer selected the items, and one at a time, moved through the room and presented them to the seated council attendees. McKee stood above them, holding the chest and smiling proudly. The British soldiers in attendance stood also, arms folded, barely disguised looks of contempt on their faces.

"Oha!" Little Turtle said. "You, McKee will send a message pf our thanks to the Great King across the sea for his gifts. Now I ask the Colonel or any of these in their fine red coats a question. In what way will these baubles be of use in the war that even our children know is soon to come? Will they fit in our musket barrels? Can they be made into arrow shafts or bows of Osage orange? Can they be eaten by our braves should a siege occur?" He raised his voice and faced directly in McKee's direction. "Along with your message of our thanks, will you ask the Great One for muskets that do not break, not the cheap trade guns that do not shoot far? Also request of him, or of someone, powder and lead. These things we desire. We must have them if victory be ours!" He sat down when the interpreter finally concluded.

The assembled braves stirred and muttered among themselves. Two Birds, a Seneca perhaps thirty years of age, suddenly jumped up. He drew back one arm and hurled his medal into the darkness outside of the open door. There was hissing and clicking of tongues for such a rude gesture, but not by many.

McKee showed some alarm as Chief Little Turtle rose to his feet once more. "Some little birds have told me that you British are building a great fortress north of here on the banks of the Mau-a-Mia River. This is good news. I wish to hear from your lips, McKee, if those little birds speak the truth. If so, what is the purpose of this fort? We would hope that it is to provide a place of refuge for your red brothers, should the battle with the mad general not go well for us. We assume that our warriors could move north and enter the fort, safe from the American canon. Is this what the little birds are telling me?"

"It is true, great chief! I, Colonel Alexander McKee, speak for all the British officers and men. It is our belief, and I assume yours as well, that no such retreat will be necessary, but should this unlikely event come to pass, the great log doors and bastions will be open to any in need!"

"It is well," Little Turtle stated, sitting once more.

"In order to further relieve your mind Chief Little Turtle, these Redcoats and I invite you and any others you choose to visit Fort Miami three days from today. I believe your other major war chief, Blue Jacket, will be there as well. We shall then counsel together."

There were murmurs of appreciation and relief from nearly all present.

Little Turtle was not so sure.

*　　　　*　　　　*

"Keep your voice down, Cas!" Tom hissed. They were sitting in a clump of young birch trees, close enough to be able to observe any movement on the trail. "Give me your knife. I'll have to cut these lashings off. Your ankles and wrists have swelled so much the knots are out of sight."

"Finally!" Big Cas growled. "Everything has gone numb. Help me stand up, Bluefoot. You wouldn't have had to keep me trussed up like this all this time. Being careful is o.k., but this has gone <u>too far!"</u>

"Stay down for a while yet. We have to be sure those four or any other Indians don't catch us like this. We wouldn't be able to bluff our way out of it this time!"

Rubbing his ankles, Cas spoke in low tones. "What am I to do for all the time that you two are in the Indian camp? We got hardly no grub and I can't risk firing my rifle even if some critter was to come by. I don't like this here plan for me."

"He's right, Tom," Sean agreed, his voice hardly audible. "I'm sorry Tom, but I don't know if I can walk much farther. I'm burning up! And I've got the awfulest headache you could ever imagine. Maybe I should stay here with Caswell. Then in a day or two him and me could make it to the place where you said Cas was to meet us."

"No! We're going into Little Turtle's village tomorrow. You can lean on me, and if that don't work I'll make a travois and drag you. The two of us have to show up there. You can bet that Bear and his companions will be passing the word about us. We have to be seen in that village."

"But," said Cas, "there should be three of us. What are you going to tell them about your 'prisoner'? Meaning me?"

Tom did not hesitate. "I'll tell them you chewed through the rawhide in the night, took 'my' rifle and ran off."

"But what am I really going to be doing? I promised the General I'd see you two no-goods to the Injun camps and get you back again. Now you know I been knowed to tell a fib once in a while. I like a little corn liquor when I can find some, and I've beat up a couple guys some times. But, I ain't never failed to take orders and do my duty. So how am I supposed to do that while I'm hiding out by some crick you told me of?"

"You're right Cas," Tom said. "I've been giving this a lot of thought. I've got a better idea. When I was a kid living with my aunt next to Little Turtle's wegiwa I used to wander around along the river. I found this big hollow tree. It was a hi-see-ni. I think you whites call them sycamores. Well you won't believe me, but that tree was hollow. I used to get inside and when I stood in the middle I couldn't touch the sides with my arms out like this." He stood and made a span of his arms. "I don't care if you believe me or not, but that's the truth of it."

"Bluefoot, I believe you about that big tree. Matter of fact I seen a hollow one bigger than what you're telling. Back in Virginny we had neighbors a couple miles down the pike. Their kid and me was pals, least when we wasn't fightin' each other. Well they had a holler sycamore like that. They'd cut a little door in the side. My pal wanted us to sleep in there but his ma kept her settin' hens in it, so it stunk real bad of chicken dabbins! Haw, haw."

Tom motioned for quiet. They all heard it then. Something was moving near the trail. Sean saw it first. It was an opossum ambling through the bushes, making no attempt to be quiet. "Just an old 'possum," Sean said, breathing normally once more. He used a bit of cloth to wipe at the yellowish seepage below his injured eye. "What's that big tree got to do with anything, Tom?"

Bluefoot cautiously stood up. He spent several minutes looking and listening. Finally he said, "I think it's o.k. to move on now, but we better keep watch for a while. Old Bear is a sly one, and may come after us yet!"

"Well what about that big tree you was talking about, Bluefoot? I ain't aiming to do no climbing if that's what's in your bonnet," Caswell said, glancing back along the trail.

"It would do fine, Cas," Tom said. "even as big as you are. There's a crack you could squeeze through. Once you get inside there'll be plenty of room. Also the good thing is you can see a little bit of the village from there. That way you might even be able to tell what's going on across the river."

"Just like a treed 'coon, is it?" Cas growled. "And what am I supposed to do all the time you and Red is sashaying around with the chiefs and the Redcoats? And what will I have to eat? I like my vittles!"

Before he answered, Tom cast a careful eye on Sean O'Casey. Even though they hadn't been walking long, the young soldier was breathing hard and what was left of his ragged shirt was plastered with sweat. It was obvious that the Private could not go on much longer.

"This is what I think will work, Caswell. You can sleep in the hollow tree during the day, then maybe get out at night for water. There are Indian gardens all around the village. You might be able to steal some food if you're careful. Then every other night or so I'll bring you whatever I can get away with. My aunt's hut is just across the river a little way."

"Sean here is about done in," Cas mused. "Maybe we better just sneak off this blasted trail a ways and camp for a while. Give him time to get over that sickness."

"We don't dare do that!" Tom hissed. "We told those Senecas we were bringing you in. We'll have to be there by tomorrow or you can bet they will be out looking for us. We've got no choice. Caswell, you better leave us now. You won't have a problem finding that tree. It's the tallest and biggest one on this side of the river. When you get it in sight, hide in the brush till dark. You'll have no trouble getting inside. The crack goes almost clear to the ground. Better get going."

Cas was far from convinced. He didn't like the plan, and he was even more apprehensive about being that close to thousands of savages, who would greatly enjoy watching him take two or three days to die! "What about him?" the big man asked, casting a critical eye on the suffering private. "I ain't about to go carrying him back to the army, and I sure don't aim to share my tree with no sick soldier!"

"I'll make that travois for him. There's no reason to conceal our tracks any more. I'll pull him along until he gets well enough to walk some more. His being so sick should help Blue Jacket and Little Turtle's warriors believe our story."

Caswell was standing over Tom, appearing to check the load on his rifle. Suddenly, with no warning at all, he swung the heavy weapon at Tom's head. The barrel struck just above Bluefoot's ear, opening a gash almost to his eyebrow. The scout went down without a sound.

"What's going on, Caswell?" Sean croaked. "Why'd you knock him out for? You gonna kill us?"

"No I ain't! Bluefoot saved my life onct so now I probly saved hisn. You two got to convince the heathens that I got loose and took the gun. He'll have a deuce of a headache but not even old Bear will doubt that there had been a fracas! Now I'm leaving. Don't you forget about your old pal hiding in that there sycamore. You hear?" He parted the bushes and without a further word disappeared, heading west toward the river.

* * *

Chief Roundhead mounted his favorite mouse-gray pony and without a backward glance headed west where many warriors were gathering by the salt lick near green leaf crossing. His horse nickered eagerly, wanting to drink at the small salt-water pool. Roundhead yanked the mare away, fearing that if the animal took too much salt she would bloat.

The Wyandot chiefs Leatherlips and Seeks Him joined forces. Both minor chiefs carried new-looking muskets from Detroit, courtesy of the British. Half their other warriors had similar weapons or trade guns. Only a handful were armed with bows, knowing they would be practically useless against the soldiers behind the fortification's log walls.

They were unaware that General Wayne had named the new position Fort Recovery. It would have made no difference if they did. Their goal was simple enough; win the battle with the hated Shemanese and scatter new bones over the graves of those from St. Clair's army, defeated in 1791, three years before.

The heat was intense near the end of June, 1794. Many of the mounted Indians preferred to walk, uncomfortable with the sweating beasts beneath them, but their spirits could not have been higher. The victory would be quick and easy. Scalps, plunder, even several cannon would be theirs! Roundhead himself was optimistic. "What does it matter that Little Turtle plans to dessert us," he asked Seeks Him, riding by his side. "We will carry our booty into his camp in triumph! Let them feel shame at choosing to ignore the fight against the Mad General and his officers. We will ride into the villages with pride!"

"It may be," Leatherlips remarked, "that we will be asked to man the new fort on the Mi-ami-si River. Should we indeed capture the soldiers' cannon there is no doubt that we would be welcomed there as heroes!"

On June thirtieth, two days later, their outriders signaled that the fort was in sight. A great number of still new-looking graves added to the attackers' confidence. The foolish Americans had re-visited the site of the previous great defeat, and incredibly, had erected ramparts almost on the bones of their departed! The spirits of the fallen could

could not have been happy about such a sacrilege, further assuring the Indians that victory would be theirs.

Small Trap, a Wyandot and close friend of Chief Roundhead, was known as a courageous, if sometimes reckless warrior. Unable to wait for orders, he charged directly at the few soldiers guarding the army corral. One of the sentries fired a hurried, ineffective shot at the apparition racing toward them, then all three fled toward the north wall's open gate. Their shouts quickly alerted those troops manning the walls. Immediately musket barrels were thrust through the loopholes on the north face. The huge gate was slammed shut and double-barred with squared timbers of black ash. Once again Wayne's unending discipline was evident as the soldiers quickly and efficiently manned their posts, muskets primed and ready.

No order was given to begin firing, but three shots fired almost simultaneously, jerked Small Trap off his feet, his right arm shredded and useless.

Roundhead urged his horse forward at a gallop. Several braves, entranced by the sight of some forty fine-looking horses now milling unprotected in the corral, were also heading that way. Roundhead shouted a command to stop this foolishness before others might decide to follow. By sheer force of will the Chief managed to prepare his troops for an attack on the fort, but the advantage of surprise was lost to the Indians. All gates were closed and the Shemanese were more than ready to defend themselves.

With gestures and a series of sharp whistles, Roundhead ordered his warriors back into the trees, out of small arms range. There was no time to waste. One of the sub-chiefs dashed up and began shouting even before he dismounted. "See! See!" he yelled pointing at the blockhouse situated on the northwest corner of the fort. Those who had not yet noticed were alerted at once. "The great gun now looks at us! There! See it?" His terror was obvious as the cannon was rolled out and prepared to fire. A Wyandot squatting near the shouting brave stood up and knocked him down with a single blow from the poll end of his war axe. Roundhead nodded approval.

There was no panic, but all those in command knew that an assault must come quickly if there would be any chance of success. Simple orders were issued. Strategy was not important, as all knew they must somehow breach the walls and get inside. There was no question that they could prevail in hand-to-hand fighting.

At Roundhead's order, those who had horses were told to dismount. Their chief knew that a brave's horse was prized above all that he owned, even his wife if he had one. If there was to be a chance for success, all efforts and every thought must be about getting over the walls, and it must be now!

With a wave of his arm Chief Roundhead led the charge, angling toward the northeast corner, away from the cannon. Such courage and bravery by his warriors made their chief's heart swell with pride. Many out-ran him as they crossed the stump-covered ground which had been cleared to provide an open field of fire.

A command was given and a coordinated volley of musketry cut through the running Indians' lines. Four went down, one killed and three badly wounded. Hardly any of the attackers noticed the slow, deliberate swing of the cannon's mouth. With a roar and a belch of smoke the gun sounded off. The aim was not yet accurate, causing most of the lethal lead balls to fly screaming over the Indians' heads. Still, two were killed, both shot through the head. Knowing that once again there was danger of panic, their chief signaled for a retreat. Another warrior was killed while attempting to drag a wounded comrade to safety.

The cannon sounded again as Roundhead's troops ran for safety. The grapeshot ripped through branches and tore into tree trunks. No one was hurt, but this time the psychological damage was significant!

Three more assaults were attempted over the following two days, two with the addition of fire arrows. All were failures. The soldiers suffered few casualties, but the Indians managed to capture a significant number of horses, and kill many more.

Would the attack have been successful if Little Turtle and Blue Jacket had lent support? No one could tell.

Tired and discouraged, Roundhead led the remaining troops north. The battle was lost.

* * *

Big Cas had not gone far when he stopped to pick up a dropped piece of rawhide, part of the very thongs with which he had been bound. "Mercy!" he whispered to himself. "Look at them big tracks my old brogans is leaving. I better do something about that for shore!" He sat down and removed the size fourteen army boots. With the laces tied together he stood up, hung the shoes around his neck, and moved off gingerly, favoring his bare feet. "If a blasted Redskin comes across my trail now, mebbe he'll think it's from a Injun that has lost his moccasins. Haw, haw! Still, I better keep a mighty careful eye out from here on. Their villages ain't more than five or six miles west. Them devils could be out hunting right near where I'm at!" He stopped a minute and peered carefully in all directions. Seeing nothing amiss he plodded on, but now he took advantage of any cover that appeared in his direction.

The more he thought about what had happened since the three of them had started on their trek, the more he hated the part he was supposed to play. "That there Bluefoot," he told himself, carefully skirting an area of soft earth, "he said if there's trouble, you was supposed to put yourself in the other guy's shoes. Well supposin' that scout's still got it in for me? Why soon as I gets all set up in that holler tree he could sic the savages onto me, and no way to escape! I better do some real serious thinking on this whole sityation."

Caswell was traveling much more slowly and carefully now, but his mind was moving at top speed. He reached into the small pouch that Bear had left with them. It was empty. "I can't believe I already et all that pemmican. That's another thing," he thought. "I ain't about to depend on them two for no vittles. That's if the Irishman's still living. They're likely to forget all about me, especially since it's gonna be mighty dangerous for them to meet me that close to the Injun camps. Well I don't intend to starve myself! I ain't seen no Injun sign at all, so I'll keep an eye out for a deer or a possum or something. I can risk taking a shot better now than when I get closer to their towns. Been noticing plenty of deer tracks, so might see one directly."

He began to take a few steps, stop and listen, then a few more. "I ain't going to hide in that tree more than two days. If I get a deer I won't need to jerk the venison. I'll just boost a haunch right into that old sycamore with me. Might even be able to have a fire in there if I'm careful about any smoke. Them Redskins would see that for shore! So, two days, no more." He continued moving west, trying to avoid open ground wherever possible.

The yearling leaped over a fallen log and looked in every direction, its ears flipping forward and back. A more experienced hunter would have been alerted to the signs immediately, but Cas was a poor woodsman. He quickly checked the priming on his rifle. Covering the lock with his hat muffled the click as he drew the hammer back and took aim. He pulled the set trigger and was prepared to fire when the small doe leaped three feet straight in the air and dashed away, a feathered arrow protruding from its flank.

Cal sank silently to the ground, sweating profusely. With infinite care he lowered the rifle's hammer, then slid full length under some bushes. Luckily for him the Indian was interested only in following his quarry. Cal could see the brave at times as he moved in a crouch, following the deer's occasional blood spoor. Caswell waited another half hour before cautiously rising from his hiding place. He was glad no one was there to see how his hands were shaking. "Well Somebody up there is shore enough looking out for an old sinner like me!" he thought. "Maybe I'd better say a couple 'thees and thous' like Bluefoot does!" He laughed at himself but it was not a very convincing laugh.

It took nearly two hours for the big soldier to cover the three remaining miles to the river. For the first time he had been made aware of the terrible danger he was in. Alone, without food, and practically in the camp of nearly four thousand armed and angry warriors, his predicament was dire indeed!

With great relief he finally spotted the giant sycamore. Even at a distance the crack was visible, starting a few feet off the ground and continuing upward for quite a distance. Cal hunkered down beside a rotten log to wait for twilight. He had no desire to be in sight trying to squeeze himself inside the tree. As Tom had said, several wegiwas were plainly visible on the opposite shore, perhaps a quarter of a mile distant. Peering through the rushes in the fading light, he even saw an Indian woman carrying a trade kettle. She was coming for water from the river.

Soon enough he would try to slip into the hollow tree. It seemed like a safe refuge, but he knew it could become his prison as well!

*   *   *

Sean groaned softly as the travois bumped across still another root. He was a very sick soldier. They were being “escorted” toward Little Turtle’s village by the five Potawatomie braves who had encountered them within sight of the largest of the several towns on the Miami River.

“Not too close!” Tom said sharply. “He may be afflicted with the white man’s spotted sickness!” The young Indian jumped back quickly, casting a frightened eye on the white man riding the travois. The four others moved back as well.

“You claim to be known to Chief Little Turtle,” one of the warriors said as they marched along. “How can we know if this is true? Suppose we were to take you directly to his wegiwa. Would you, a puny Wyandot, be so proud then?”

“Also,” stated another, “why do you bring the sick Shemanese to our camps? He does not have the spots of what the whites call ‘the pox’. Any fool can see that this man has been whipped! It is only the white soldiers who sometimes bear such scars. You are lying!” He turned to the others, causing the procession to stop. “Let us kill them both right now! We can cast peach pits to see who gets the scalps. No one is going to believe their story anyway.”

A second Potawatomi agreed immediately. "Wise words," he stated emphatically. "Also, we can make up a tale of how we vanquished these two after a long and dangerous fight!" The others laughed aloud at the joke.

"I see my friend and I are in the power of some very shrewd captors," Tom stated calmly. "Certainly you could easily kill us, as it is five warriors against two who are unarmed, one of them very sick. Yes, it would take real courage to put us to death. What a story you could tell around the council fire during the scalp dance! Of course each of you must be sure to tell exactly the same lie, or your 'reward' would become nothing but derisive laughter. As my uncle and friend, Black Pipe, often said, 'a liar must have a good memory'!"

Tom's taunts earned him a sharp strike from the handle of a war club. Deliberately well placed, the blow started the blood seeping from his wounds again.

One of the braves, who had not yet spoken, stopped their progress again. "You claim to know the great Miami chief, Little Turtle. Now you mention Black Pipe. It is clear that you have spent time among some of our people. Perhaps you are telling the truth. We shall see. But know this: if what you are trying to convince us of proves to be only an attempt to save your life, believe me when I assure you that your death will not be a quick one! I have spoken!"

For the first time, Sean pushed himself up a little and tried to speak. "Tell them I don't have no smallpox, Tom. You know I don't. Get them to . . .to . . .take us right to the chief's house . . .where . . . you can . . ." His voice faltered and he fell back against the travois, coughing.

Quickly, Tom wiped away the mucous from his friend's eye, then answered the brave who had just spoken. "My friend asks me to insist that we be taken directly to your chief, just as we have been saying. He doesn't have the pox or any other sickness. He needs a healer, or I fear he will soon die. Then the information he could give to your chiefs about the American army would be lost! We could move faster if one of you would take one side of the sled and help me pull. This man has important information that your war chiefs need to hear. He is a deserter directly from the army of the Mad General. He will tell it all and I will be his interpreter. If he dies, or you kill us, this information will be lost. The war chiefs will not look kindly on any of you should that happen!"

The Potawatomis looked uncertain. One of them finally did grab the other side of the sled. The progress was much faster then. "Why was this man whipped so much that his eye was blinded?" one asked.

"He hated the General's cruel treatment of his troops. He threatened to tell me the battle plans for the coming war with your people," Tom lied easily. "We both were beaten, and with all the soldiers watching. Does it surprise you that we ran away? While hiding in the forest, we even captured a Shemanese soldier, but he escaped from us. If only you five had arrived earlier you would have had a real prize for the stake!"

A scattering of bark shelters came into view. Tom could not help glancing along the river to the south. His view was rewarded. The great sycamore towered over the other trees, not far from where they stood, waiting for a canoe to cross and ferry them over. It took two trips, since Sean still could not sit up.

A crowd was quickly gathering. Several small boys grabbed sticks and began to hit and prod at Sean until one of the braves ordered them aside. The procession headed toward the center of the village, Tom nearly carrying his half-conscious friend. Sean's red hair proved to be an object of wonder, especially for the young women in the crowd.

"Soon," said one of the Potawatomis, "we shall see if any of these claims of yours are true or not." He spoke briefly to one of the four braves and the procession stopped not far from a large, almost square lodge. At that very moment an imposing figure emerged. Clothed in doeskin leggings and a white man's shirt, Little Turtle stepped into the evening light. He glanced at the gathering near his home but did not approach.

"Great Chief," the leader of the Potawatomis said politely, "we beg a few minutes of your time. May we enter your dwelling?"

Little Turtle turned, opened the door flap and spoke a few words to those within. "It is hot inside," the chief then said. "Let us sit by the river. Come."

When all were seated a pipe was passed to each and they smoked. Little Turtle still had shown no notice whatever of Tom and Sean. The Potawatomis were casting furious glances at the scout.

Finally Little Turtle handed his pipe to a waiting woman, turned and looked full in Tom's face. "Toom-She-chi-Kwa, you have become a man. I believe it has been three winters since you were last with us. Why have you come back to us at this time?" Not only the five Potawatomis, but indeed nearly all who were watching were amazed at this turn of events. Tom could not help flashing a triumphant look at his captors.

"Yes, Great Chief, it has been several years. I am grateful that you remember me after all this time. I have returned with a shameful face! I had been a scout for the general they call 'mad'. Having come to my senses I decided to desert the paleface army. I was caught, whipped, and put in irons. It is my hope that you and your fellow chiefs can forgive an errant fool and accept the information that my friend and I have to give. I am at your mercy."

Little Turtle sat unmoving, his attention apparently upon a wedge of geese winging their way south. At length he asked another question. "You were whipped by the Shemanese soldiers? I see evidence of a severe whipping on the white man who accompanies you. But where are your wounds?"

Tom stood, loosened the shirt Sean had given him, then carefully pulled it over his head. A gasp rose from the lookers. The chief nodded, got slowly to his feet, and spoke a few words. "Tomorrow when the sun is halfway up the sky, you will come to my wegiwa. I will hear your words." He motioned to a waiting brave. "See that the white man is taken to the healer. Keep him under guard for three days."

*   *   *

Private Caswell rose to his knees and spent a long moment looking in all directions. The near darkness gave him confidence, but he knew that being this close to the enemy, he must be very cautious. Still not standing erect, he crept forward until he was close enough to touch the huge trunk. Like all of this species, the sycamore's bark was a mottled white and brown. From Cas' view it was nearly all white, causing it to stand out sharply against the surrounding forest.

"Well Caswell," he told himself grimly, "there's just no other way for it. I'll have to get out of these dirty buckskins or I'll show up like a bear in a snowbank!"

Stripped to the skin, he rolled up his clothes, and stood up, leaning against the tree. "Guess I'd better shove my duds in there first, then my shoes," he told himself. Everything went in easily enough, but the more he examined the crack, the more it seemed to look too narrow. "Reckon I'll lose some hide getting in there," he thought. But with all his clothes now inside the hollow tree he was committed. It appeared that the higher the crack rose on the trunk the wider the opening became. In no way however, did it appear the gap was as big as he would need. "That lousy Stink Foot! Him being skinny as a fence rail, it's no wonder he could slip in and out of this here opening. And," he continued to think, "he wasn't even full growed up back then!"

His mother had always said that there was "no sense crying over spilled milk." He nudged one foot in the bottom of the fissure. Feeling not only fearful, but ridiculous as well, he swung himself up until he was even with the widest opening. With this head and one shoulder inside, he had no trouble wriggling the rest of his body into the complete darkness within. Hoping he did not land on a bobcat or a porcupine, he dropped to the floor. His bare feet met all sorts of debris. Leaves, dried up animal droppings, and who knew what else, did not bother him at all. What did cause near panic was being completely enclosed in such a small dark space. Even when a child, probably because of his unusual size, even then, he had always felt uncomfortable when confined in any way.

The shouts of the drill sergeant were forever stored in his memory. So before he even put on clothes and shoes, by touch alone he checked the prime and load in his rifle. Scraping up some of the trash at his feet he boosted himself up until he had a moonlight view from his lair. Much had happened during the last eighteen hours. For this reason he was able to lean back against the smooth inside of the tree and instantly fall asleep.

Morning light was filtering in when he awoke. Hunger gnawed at his stomach, but there was nothing he could do about it until evening when he expected Tom to sneak him some vittles. "He better not forget me!" he murmured aloud. "If he don't show up by moonrise I'm climbing back out of here. I'll head south to meet up with the soldiers, no matter what this crazy mission was supposed to be!"

Cas found a way to sort of wedge himself upright, one eye at the narrow opening near the bottom of the crack. His prized rifle was leaning well within his reach, but he was not about to thrust the muzzle into view.

In just a few minutes he saw what appeared to be the same woman coming for water. Other women and children appeared on the far bank moving about doing chores or playing. Two little boys entered the water, splashing and leaping about. Cas was grateful for the sight of anything moving. It helped pass the time, as well as taking his mind off his growling, empty stomach. Thankfully no warriors had appeared.

Slowly time passed. In late afternoon he slept again. After pushing the accumulation of trash to the west side of the enclosure, he gained a precarious footing further up, where he could command a wider view.

Suddenly he heard voices, apparently from behind his tree! Two little girls came into view below and to his left. Cautiously he moved his head a little way back from the opening, still keeping them in sight. They came closer. The taller of the two moved to the very base of the tree. Cas broke into a sweat. He attempted to quiet his breathing as the child appeared to be examining the hole. He could not understand a word of their almost constant chatter, but the closest one then motioned with one hand. There was no need to understand their language! He saw immediately that the taller girl was asking the other to boost her up so she could see into the hollow tree! With hardly a second to plan, Cas yanked off his black slouch hat, held it over his face, and waited. The girl's face appeared, not six inches from his own. Very slowly the soldier moved a few inches closer to the child's smiling face.

"OWWWOOOOO!" he moaned, only slightly above a whisper. Shock and terror flashed across her countenance. She sprang backward, screaming. In a heartbeat both girls were crashing through the bushes toward the river. Cas' heart was hammering as he watched them splash through the shallows until the water was deep enough for swimming. Floundering up the far bank, they finally stopped and stared back toward his hiding place. Now was the crucial moment! He grabbed his kit and rifle, held his shoes at the ready, and waited to see what they would do. "If them two goes running and yelling into their village I'm leaving this hole!" He told himself. They did not run. He could plainly see them conversing desperately, casting frightened glances back at the big tree across the river. Finally, hand in hand, they strolled out of sight among the lodges.

"Looks like they decided nobody's gonna believe them, and everybody would think them just scared little children!" Cas thought. He decided that for the moment at least he was probably safe.

* * *

"Toom-She-chi-Kwa it is good that you have returned to us. It is my desire that you stay with me unless the chiefs have other plans for you." Tom's aunt did not appear any older than she had three years before. "It is said," she continued, "that your father, my brother, lives beside the new fort they call Fort Malamia. It is but a day's journey form here. Would you wish to go there and try to find him? I would go with you." A look of disgust crossed her wrinkled face. "If we do find him he will probably be drunk or off begging for strong drink. Bah!"

I cannot go today, Auntie. Chief Little Turtle has ordered me to his lodge in late morning. I would very much like to see my father however. Perhaps tomorrow or the day after."

"Do not be surprised when you see him. He is but a shell of the fine man he once was. He was here last hunger moon, seeking anything I had that he could sell. When he first arrived in my village he did not even recognize me, his own sister! Have you heard the name the children gave him?"

"No, I have only just arrived. It must not be an honorable name."

"They always gathered around him and kept repeating, 'Tay-neh-iss-nah'!"

Tom was embarrassed and saddened. "He Who Falls Down A Lot" was not a name to be proud of. "The Shemanese are the fault of my father's misfortune," he stated angrily. "They give our people whiskey, then take everything from us. It has been so with all the treaties the whites have made. When I was a scout for the Mad General's army the soldiers laughed at how easy it has been to cheat us and our ancestors in this way."

Tom's aunt clucked her tongue but did not offer a response to his statements. For a long moment she stared at the young man, then bade him sit on the bench against the wall.

"I must speak what is on my mind, nephew," she began firmly. I know that you are well aware that Seven Sisters, the mother of Takes The Belt, had lost two sons, a nephew, and her husband in a raid three years ago. You do know this do you not?"

Tom nodded. He had a good idea what she was driving at, and it was not what he wanted to hear. "Please continue," he said politely.

"Who could blame Seven Sisters for desiring revenge for the loss of nearly her entire family? No one! The small Shemanese girl, the one with two braids, was to be hers in payment for her loss. All was in readiness. The little white girl was to be put to the stake the following noon. Do you remember all of this?"

"Yes, Auntie, it was some time ago, but I know about it."

"Perhaps you do not know, however, that someone killed the child in the night, thus robbing Seven Sisters of her rightful vengeance." She did not speak for several minutes but stared intently into Tom's eyes. He said nothing.

At length she continued. "When you were taken to our chief's wegiwa did you see there a young man about your age, wearing a mantle of fox fur?"

"No, my Aunt. I did not even enter Little Turtle's lodge. He came out to sit by the river, but I did hear voices from within."

"That man's name is Roamer. You may remember him.

Since you returned he has resumed his story that he knows who killed the white child. So far he has not told the name of the one he suspects. If I were that person I would be very careful when around Roamer!"

"An interesting story Auntie. Thank you for telling it. Now I must go to see the Chief. Perhaps this Roamer will be there."

"I'm sure he will," she said. "He is a great favorite of the war chiefs, so spends much time with them. Now remember this: 'the badger is not caught in the snare so long as it keeps one eye on what is behind!'"

Tom headed for the council lodge, his aunt's words still echoing in his mind. He cleared his throat loudly while still outside the imposing structure's door flap. The young man who admitted him was undoubtedly the very one about whom his aunt had warned him.

"You may enter," Roamer said, pleasantly enough. He eyed Tom Bluefoot at length as they moved toward the tiny council fire. It was then that Tom was surprised to see a gathering of visitors. Seated before several of the chiefs, were none other than Blue Jacket and Alexander McKee. Roamer indicated that Toom-She-chi-Kwa be seated, well to the back.

Tom assumed a casual air as he examined the one who might be his accuser. A handsome brave, Roamer was dressed in what could only be described as elegant clothing. He was well muscled and of handsome features. Taller and heavier than Tom, He had the appearance of one well satisfied with himself!

McKee was speaking. "It is as you say, Chief Little Turtle. Your British brothers are well aware of your soldiers' needs for better guns and much more powder and lead. As your friend and ally it is my wish that all this and more be supplied to you without fail. Unfortunately the recent war with the American General, Washington, has left us badly depleted." He stopped speaking, waiting for the translation.

Tom was amazed when he saw Blue Jacket rise and face the assembly. He began to translate, but it very soon became apparent that he had forgotten much of his childhood language. After numerous glaring errors he made one which could result in disaster. "The Colonel says he will supply better guns, powder, and lead, since the war with the Americans is over."

Tom suddenly stood up. "Great Chiefs," he began, "I am of no repute, only a deserter from the Mad General's army. However I was raised by a white man. I can speak both their language and ours. May I be of service as interpreter?"

The resounding slap reverberated off the bark walls. Tom's head snapped back as hisses and growls emerged from the enraged gathering. Roamer drew back his hand, preparing to deliver another blow for this unheard of breach of etiquette and protocol.

"Enough!" It was Blue Jacket who spoke. "It has been many years since I had to use the words of the Shemanese. The lad may be right. He can be of help. Colonel McKee can verify whatever is interpreted by this man. Bring him near to me. Is all that has happened acceptable to you Chief Little Turtle?"

"It is. Let us continue. So, Colonel McKee you are saying that the soldiers at Detroit can be of little help to us in the coming battle?"

Tom translated rapidly. Both McKee and Blue Jacket listened very carefully. Satisfied, they indicated that Tom should be the interpreter for the rest of the day. There were a few smiles as those assembled could see that the work could now continue much more smoothly. One was not smiling! Roamer's face was mottled with rage. Tom knew it would take all his vigilance to avoid a confrontation with that man!

Thanks to a more efficient interpreter, important plans were soon made regarding each tribe's part in the battle. The gathering broke up in late afternoon. Little Turtle was obviously worried. He had hoped and assumed that the British would not only supply trained troops, but even several canon for the Indians' aid in the coming battle with Mad Anthony Wayne's army. Scouts had urgent reports of the nearness of the Americans. Surely it would be only a matter of days until the attack came. Blue Jacket and several of the lesser chiefs displayed a confident air. Had they not only won great battles against both St. Clair and Harmar, and with very little loss of life? Little Turtle and some of his closest companions were not convinced.

As quickly as good manners and protocol allowed, Tom hurried into the fading sunlight. It had been too long for Big Cas to go with very little food. "I must get all I can and deliver it before full darkness tonight," he told himself. "But first I'll see if they will let me visit Sean in the healer's hut."

After asking directions Tom soon arrived at the small dwelling.

Outside, all sorts of strange objects dangled from the lodge poles. A buffalo skull, a cluster of what appeared to be bird beaks, and deer antlers were some of the things that Tom recognized. The healer evidently believed in advertising!

"I wish to enter," Tom said politely. Almost immediately the elk skin was thrown back. Tom nearly stepped backward in fright. A small, dark Indian stood in the entrance. He was dressed in a blue blanket, obviously of British manufacture, but what Tom could not help noticing was that the man had only one eye! The Indian Toom-she-chi-Kwa was confronting was no other than the one known as "The Prophet", brother of Tecumseh! The man did not speak at all, but motioned for Tom to enter. The small dwelling was half filled with some sort of aromatic smoke. The heat was truly stifling. The healer seemed to be in some sort of trance, but his lips were moving as if in prayer. The Prophet stood unmoving, arms folded, his only eye missing nothing. Tom placed a hand on his friend's forehead. Thankfully the fever seemed to be gone. "How are you feeling?" he asked.

"That you Tom? Thank God you're here! They ain't give me nothing to eat but some kind of soup or medicine that I had all I could do to keep down! This old guy with one eye out has really been a help to me. I guess he knows what it's like to lose an eye. I don't know who he is, and we can't understand one another, but he got rid of my guards right away. He's been here ever since."

Tom was elated to hear Sean talking in such a strong voice. It appeared that he was nearly well. His wounded eye was bound with a piece of trade cloth, no seepage discoloring it. With a start, the healer suddenly leaped to his feet and began vigorously shaking a turtle shell rattle around Sean's head. His almost inaudible chanting was interrupted by a statement from The Prophet.

"You are his friend, and you are of our people," he said somberly. "Do you then speak our tongue?"

"Yes, great warrior. All, both white and red have heard much of your powers. You, the brother of Tecumseh, are well known!"

"Oha!" The Prophet responded. "Your friend is much improved. He will lose his eye. Our healer has done well in such a short time with this white man, but the eye is gone, like mine was many years ago. The eye must be removed."

After thanking The Prophet, again Tom spoke to his friend. His message was urgent, but he kept his words calm, even making it sound as if he was simply joking with the Irishman.

"If you can travel we've got to get out of here tonight! There's a brave here who is pretty sure it was me who killed that little girl three years ago. He saw me run away that time. He'll keep an eye on both of us, I'm sure." Tom laughed and patted Sean on the shoulder, continuing his charade. "I'm going to get some food to Cas tonight. Then we better head south from the big sycamore Cas is in. Do you think you can get away?" Tom laughed again as if a great joke had been told. Sean joined in.

"I'll get away all right. I've been making them think I can't walk, but except for my eye I'm as good as new. After marching and drilling for nearly a year and a half, a few days lying around won't be no trouble! We better quit talking now or the other one-eyed man in this hut will get suspicious. I'll be hiding near Cas' tree as soon as it's full dark. I'll meet you there."

"Good! We'll make a run for it," Tom laughed, nodding to The Prophet as he left the healer's hut.

He fought the urge to run. Twilight was near and Talks Little's wegiwa sat at the far end of the village. He hurried inside, pleased to see a wooden bowl of stew ready on her small table. She was smoking a pipe, not unlike the one which was her husband's namesake. True to her name, she spoke little as her nephew gobbled the cold food. When the bowl was empty she handed him a packet of buckskin tied with a cord. "What's this?" Tom asked in surprise.

"It is for your journey," she stated simply. "The one called Roamer, of whom I warned you, was here looking for you while you were visiting the red haired one. He had murder in his eye! You must run! Tonight! Now!"

Tom shoved the bundle under his shirt, gripped the old woman's arm with both his hands and slipped outside. It took all his will power to keep from dashing toward the river. He kept up a normal pace, even humming to himself until he was at the edge of the stream. Trying to look unconcerned, he glanced about. Seeing no one, he stepped into the shallows. Tom knew that entering the water fully clothed would certainly be noticed by anyone in the area.

The current was strong. With water up to his waist he was stopped by a shout!

"Stop, traitor! Another step and I will shoot you dead!"

Roamer also entered the river, keeping his rifle trained on Tom's middle. The gun he held was not one of the cheap, unreliable things perpetrated on the Indians by both English and American traders. It was a fine piece, of French manufacture. At less than twenty paces he could not miss

"You are mistaken!" Tom yelled desperately. "I am no traitor. I am a friend of Little Turtle and his interpreter as well. Put down your weapon." The light was fast fading. Tom felt if he could keep Roamer talking a little longer he would dive under and swim as fast as he could.

"I saw you run away after smothering the white child. I saw you!" I intend to only wound you at this time. After all is made clear to the chiefs I will enjoy watching you writhe and scream at the stake! The mother of the fallen ones will have her revenge at last. I am aiming at your shoulder, white lover!" Talk was over. Roamer took deliberate aim, intending to wound the scout, but suddenly, without a sound, he slid forward into the current. An instant later the boom of a powerful rifle shot echoed and re-echoed down the river. It seemed to have come from a large sycamore on the opposite bank!

The Indian warriors were all on high alert, expecting an assault by the American army at any time. Tom whirled and splashed back to shore, shouting. "The-sem- oha! The-sem-oha! The soldiers are hiding in the trees! Run! Run!" There was pandemonium in the camp. War horses were untied. Women and their youngest children ran west, away from the river.

It was a brilliant move by the Wyandot scout. He was paid no notice as he raced back to the healer's hut. Without knocking he burst inside. The healer, who had been preparing to flee himself, was astonished by the intrusion. He began to protest when his patient leaped from his pallet and shoved him crashing back into the bowls and baskets of medicine.

They separated then, but both heading for the river as fast as they could run. They entered the stream some thirty paces apart. Wading and swimming they made the crossing in what must have been record time!

"Come on, Bluefoot! Get yer britches outn that river. We need to get crackin'!"

Breathless and dripping, Tom raced up the bank. "Sean's right over there," he gasped, panting. "You got everything out of the tree?"

"Shore I do! Climbed out soon as I reloaded my rifle. That you, Red? Let's make tracks!"

"No, don't make any tracks!" Tom laughed as the three sped south down the river trail. Already they could smell smoke from the army's cooking fires. A mile, two at the most, would see them safe behind the American lines. That was if they weren't shot by one of Wayne's sentries!

Feeling they were no longer in immediate danger they slowed to a walk. How could they have known that two of Little Turtle's perimeter guards were patrolling the very part of the trail that Tom, Cas, and Sean were on? One eagle-eyed brave had seen the muzzle flash from Big Cas' rifle. He and his companion slipped into the brush to see if those approaching were friend or foe. It did not take long! Big Cas was half a head taller and a hundred pounds heavier than nearly any Indian. He was whispering excitedly. "Reckon that there varmint who was gonna shoot you is in the 'Happy Hunting Ground' right now. Haw, haw! Could you see where my bullet hit him?"

"Right below his ribs I think."

"Dang! I didn't allow for enough drop! Musta been seventy or eighty yards across that river. Next time I'll . . ."

The sudden blast nearly deafened them. Cas fell to the ground, gripping his side. The second guard took aim at Sean and pulled the trigger. There was a flash of powder but no report. "Flash in the pan" was a common occurrence with flintlocks.

Once again General Wayne's relentless training came to the fore. Sean grabbed Caswell's rifle and shot from the hip. The first Indian fell dead. The second threw his useless musket down and ran into the forest.

"Halt!" An American sentry's voice cut through the darkness.

"Don't shoot, man! It's me, big Cas, and I got Sean O'Casey and the Injun Bluefoot with me. I got a rifle ball in my belly, but I can still walk. Put your hammer down, we're a-comin' in!"

They were safe!

* * *

General Wayne was pacing nervously back and forth in the command tent. He was not, however, at all inattentive to Tom Bluefoot's words.

"A jumble of broken and uprooted trees, you say? Was it made as an attempt at fortifications by the Indians? How large would you estimate this 'jumble' to be?"

Wayne's questions came quickly, one after the other. "No sir, it's already been there for a few years. My people call it sermistika gama, 'place of the swirling wind'. I did not see it this time, as it is far from Little Turtle's village. I was only in the enemy camp a day and a night."

"Quite right, of course. Could you provide me with an estimate of the size of the destruction? Obviously the path of a tornado."

"As best I can recall, and thou must remember it has been four years since I lived with my aunt in Little Turtle's village, I would guess it would be a half hour's march in each direction."

"I see. Are the fallen trees large or small?"

"Large, sir. Very large, and lying twisted together in all directions."

"Would there be any openings in the tangle large enough for cavalry to penetrate?"

"I don't know for sure sir, but I think not."

Mad Anthony began pacing again. "I see," he said. "What do you recall of the terrain surrounding the downed trees?"

"What meanest thou, 'terrain'?"

"The land. Is it hilly? Covered with trees? Wet or dry? That sort of thing."

Tom answered confidently at once. "The land is mostly level and it is dry this time of year. There is a fine open area to the west side of the jumble where my people pasture their horses. Cavalry could be used very well there I would think."

"Another question, Tom Bluefoot, does it appear . . ."

"Begging your pardon General Wayne, but could someone see to the wounds of my friends, Privates Caswell and O'Casey? If thou would give the order the surgeon might be able to tend to their injuries."

"Caswell? Caswell?" The General stroked his chin a moment. "Is he the sharpshooter who won our impromptu shooting match?"

"That is correct sir. He was shot in the side as we made our escape from the enemy. He can walk, but not without pain.

And if I may continue, Private Sean O'Casey is in need of immediate attention."

"The soldier flogged on the same day you were?"

"Yes Sir. I think he has lost his eye."

"Orderly!" Wayne shouted. The tent flap parted almost immediately. A young officer stepped inside and saluted smartly.

'Sir?"

"Find the two recruits who came back to our lines last night. Escort them to the surgeon's quarters immediately. They are to receive first priority, regardless of any others presently being treated!"

The orderly saluted and hurried out.

"I have neglected my manners, Scout Bluefoot. I should have inquired about the health of your companions and yourself. I have been informed that the single blow from the whip unfortunately resulted in the injury of the private's eye. Is that correct?"

"It is, sir," Tom stated calmly. "It is my opinion that he has completely lost the sight in that eye. The healer who attempted to treat him while we were in Little Turtle's village said the same."

"I gave the order for the high hit," Wayne stated, staring into space. "It was done deliberately in order to give evidence to the enemy that the man had ample reason to desert. It was meant to save his life during the spying mission upon which I was I was about to send him. Neither I nor the sergeant carrying out the punishment had any intention of causing such a serious injury."

"I know that sir. And it worked very well, even to the extent that Private O'Casey was befriended and even protected by 'The Prophet', whom, as you may know, had also lost an eye!"

"The Prophet was there?" Wayne asked excitedly. "Will he be providing more warriors for the battle?"

"I do not know, sir. Thou mayest wish to interrogate Private O'Casey, who actually spent time with Tecumseh's brother. Of course they could not understand one another."

After another pause, General Wayne turned his full attention on Bluefoot. "And what of your own 'stripes'?" he asked, somewhat belatedly. "Are they healing well? The sergeant is most diligent when doing the punishments! Some of the officers tell me that the man enjoys the work overmuch!"

"They are nearly healed. Thank you General. My aunt applied some of our people's remedies, but I was not with her long enough for them to help much. I thank thee for thy concern."

"I do not apologize for my policies," the general stated firmly. "When I took command I had only what amounted to a collection of independent-thinking backwoodsmen and far too many self-appointed 'officers' who knew nothing of true soldiering. Desertion was a continuous problem. Rigorous, unfailing discipline was the answer, and only the lash would enforce it!"

Tom said nothing. What was there to say?

"Now once again I must hear what you have learned regarding the chiefs' battle plans. You may speak at will."

"Your pardon, General, but could thou grant me a few minutes to visit my comrades? I am much worried about them, especially Private O'Casey. It is my hope that the surgeon will be able to restore his sight."

"Granted. Your concern is appreciated. When you have finished, direct the big man, Private Caswell I believe, to report directly to me."

Tom soon learned that his friends had already been treated. The surgeon's tent had once been white, but after nearly two years, five different encampments, and several hundred miles of arduous travel, it appeared little different from those of the troops.

Captain Friederich Gruber was a large, gruff-speaking man whose reputation with the troops was decidedly mixed. Certainly his occupation was not for the timid! He had been with the army since the Revolution, and there was little He had not seen in the way of wounds. He had saved many lives, but many more had died, even after he'd done everything he could for them. The soldiers appreciated his attempts, but most thought that if wounded they might fare better if "Old Sawbones" just left them alone!

Sean was lying face down on a pallet against one wall, big Cas sitting up against another. "How art thou feeling, Sean?"

"No sense tryin' to talk to the redhead right now, Bluefoot," Big Cas drawled. "He's purty well in what you might call 'happy land'! Plumb full of laudanum just like I am."

"And mighty lucky to have it!" the surgeon snapped. "After the battle, there's likely to be none left. Hundreds of shot up and tomahawked boys are going to be screaming for it, and I'll probably be cutting body parts offn them with nothing to ease the pain."

"Sorry, doc. You're shorely right and I'm glad you had some for me and the redhead yonder. Lookee here, Bluefoot." Cas pulled up his shirt. Two rolled up pieces of gauze were protruding from the holes in his side, one where the bullet entered and the other where it left his lower back. "Watch this!" Caswell gripped the cloth, one end in each beefy fist. He sawed the bandage back and forth, pulling it through the path of the bullet. "Ain't that <u>something?</u> The doc run a big needle clean through there, then pulled this rag through and left it in. I'm supposed to pull it back and forth like this a couple times a day. It don't hurt hardly atall!"

"It'll hurt <u>plenty</u> tomorrow, big man! Better enjoy it while you can."

"Cas," Tom broke in, "you're supposed to report to the General. Can you walk that far?"

"Is it o.k. Doc? Can I go see the General with this here rag stickin' out of my belly?"

"Sure you can," the captain replied. "It may start bleeding again. Here's a roll of muslin. If the bleeding is bad, use a pocket knife or a smooth stick or something and push some more cloth in the hole. You planning to fight in the battle tomorrow?"

Both Tom and Cas were startled. It was the first time they had been told the actual date of the attack. "Wal I reckon I'll be right in the middle of that there fracas," Big Cas stated proudly. "Now I better get over to the General's tent and see what's in his bonnet for me. He'll probably be askin' my advice about a lot of things!"

He strode briskly from the surgeon's tent as if he had no pain whatever. Once out of sight however, he walked more slowly, and with a decided limp.

Even though there were several officers surrounding General Wayne, he welcomed Caswell cordially. "Are you well enough to join the assault in the morning?" he asked immediately.

"I <u>am</u> Sir! You've seen me shoot. Just let me put my sights on some of them thievin' redskins, then you'll see . . ."

"That's very good Private. I have a special assignment for you. Assemble the fourteen sharpshooters and give them last minute instructions. Anything you can tell them that will increase their accuracy will be helpful. In order to help with this order I am giving you a field promotion to the rank of sergeant."

"Me . . .? A real sergeant, Sir? Wal I'll be! You can count on old private, I mean sergeant Caswell to do a fine job on this here special assignment, Sir! I'll start right away. I know just what . . ."

"Dismissed!"

* * *

Little Turtle was doing all he could to appear confident, but a sense of foreboding was riding his shoulders like a wet mantle. Keeping a half smile on his face he tried valiantly to hide his disgust, not only at the young braves, that was to be expected, but even to several of the minor chiefs as well. The dancing around the scalp pole was becoming more and more frenzied. Nearly naked braves periodically left the dance to slash furiously at the post with their tomahawks. "Let us hope the Great Spirit will help these valiant warriors when it will not be a wooden pole they are attacking!" he thought grimly. "The long knives attached to the Americans' muskets will be jammed between their ribs before our axes can even be raised to strike!

Chief Little Turtle watched Blue Jacket from the corner of his eye. Resplendent in the coat which gave him his name, the Shawnee chief gave ample evidence of his elation at the prospect of the battle that was almost certain to come on the following morning. "He is doing what a real war chief must do," Little Turtle thought. "He encourages those he will lead into the fray. He is eager for the battle! Would that I could be more like him."

It was easy to see how excited all the warriors were. Their great successes against both Shemanese leaders, Harmar and St. Clair were still fresh in their minds. They could still hear the cries of the cowering soldiers as they struck them down. They could still see the mounds of dead, their scalps now hanging on the belts of nearly every Indian in the battle. But as Little Turtle maintained his artificial smile, he was thinking about those conflicts. Those Shemanese had been complete fools! In their arrogance they had not utilized their advanced scouts. Very few guards were posted around their camps, and those who were had often fallen asleep! Conducting two successful ambushes had been as child's play. Yes, as principal war chief he had shared in the pride of those victories, but in his heart he knew that this time it could be very different. The general that even the whites themselves called "Mad" meant to win this war. His intent was to end the red man's power for all time. His sentries did not sleep! If any did they were whipped almost to death. Consider the two deserters who had come to them yesterday. Both exhibited undeniable evidence of General Wayne's discipline!

The Chief's spies had been observing the American army for nearly two years. Their reports gave ample evidence of a corps of men being taught to obey orders, no matter how a conflict fared. They were constantly marching, so much so that they could travel great distances in all kinds of weather, and through the thickest forests. "These soldiers," Little Turtle told himself, "know how to fight!"

"Greetings, my Chief." Blue Jacket and two other leaders slipped to the ground near enough to Little Turtle that they could make themselves heard above the shrieks of the whirling dancers. "You do not join in the scalp dance?" one asked.

"I am far too old for that these days," he answered with a tired smile. "Is there any further word from McKee? Has he gone to Detroit to make sure the British and Canadians are on their way to help us?"

"He did not go to Detroit. At any rate it is too late for that now. It is believed that the Englishman has gone to the new fort called Miamius, near us to the north. "

"Promises, promises!" Little turtle made no effort to hide his disgust. "I have never trusted any white man, be they English or American. We were assured that better arms and even three cannon would be given to us to help when we face the mad general. What have they given? Vermillion war paint, the kind that does not come off easily. Pah!"

"Let your mind rest at ease," Blue Jacket murmured. He quickly looked about, worried that Little Turtle's pessimistic words might be heard above the revelry. Soothingly, he continued. "We do not need help from any of them! Look about you. Have you ever seen more confidence, more eagerness to meet the enemy? Have courage, great chief. You have led us to victory many times before, as have I, and these beside us as well. We will triumph once again!"

Little Turtle's smile was genuine this time. He gripped Blue Jacket's arm with both hands. "Oha!" he said. How he loved and admired these, his friends and comrades, but a little bird was asking a question in his mind. "How many of these brave men will die tomorrow?"

There was no answer.

*   *   *

Big Cas was standing uncertainly beside Wayne's tent. Summarily dismissed, he was not sure if he should round up the sharpshooters and begin his instructions or wait for a more direct order. "Well, well. Here comes this here army's favorite spies. Ain't seen you in a hour or so, haw, haw!"

Tom grinned at the big soldier, now a sergeant. "Cas, I never did thank thee properly for saving my life last night. How did thee happen to see that Indian about to shoot me? It was nearly dark, and a long way across the river."

"How could I help it? I was so hungry I'd about decided to shoot you ifn you ever showed yourself! Another thing. I hate little tight rooms like it was in that tree. Gives me the shivers! I felt better looking outn that crack. Spent a lot of time doing that there."

"It must have been a lucky shot, clear across the river like that," Sean said.

"Lucky my Aunt Sally!" Cas growled. "Guess you ain't heard yet that I'm a sergeant now!"

"Yes siree! It's me. General Wayne appointed me hisself not twenty minutes ago. I'm to instruct them others, thinks they can shoot. Well most of them couldn't hit the side of a barn ifn they was inside of it! I got a couple hours to teach them a thing or two. Haw haw!" He peered at Sean's heavily bandaged face. "How's the eye, Red?"

"I guess the eye is o.k. It's lying in the rinse bucket under the surgeon's table. Didn't hurt too bad when he cut it out, but it's sure starting to now! How about your bullet wound?"

Pulling up his shirt, Caswell sawed the long rope of bandages back and forth as he had done to show Tom. "Lucky I can be in the battle tomorrow, even if it does hurt like thunder. Without old Cas, them lazy soldiers would be bound to lose the whole affair! Watch fer a big man out in front, pickin' off redskins fast as he can load. That there will be me!" He hurried off, calling the names of those he was to train.

Sean and Tom entered Wayne's tent, almost on tiptoe. The General was writing brief notes. He handed them off to a series of couriers who ran out to find the recipients. When the tent was finally empty of runners he looked up at the two men standing motionless against the tent wall. "Sit. Both of you. I see the surgeon has dealt with your injured eye," he said, staring at the heavy bandages across Sean's forehead. "Was he able to save your sight?"

"No General, he had to remove my eye."

"I am sorry," Wayne said sincerely. "I had no intention of that happening. My intent was only to save you from the savages once you entered their villages. Whatever others may say of our Indian foes, I know that they are very shrewd and most observant. Had you and the scout not shown obvious reason to desert our army, your story would not have been believable to them. Now, Private Bluefoot, kindly give me your report. Leave nothing out, even to the smallest detail." He winced as he attempted to move his foot. As usual it was propped up on a padded powder keg.

"I am not versed in tactics at all, sir, but by serving as interpreter for the British I heard just about everything they were planning. Thou canst make of it what thou will."

"Excellent! Continue."

"First, it looked to me as if Little Turtle, chief of the Miamis, is not wholeheartedly in favor of the battle."

Wayne's head snapped forward. "Might he refuse to fight then, would you say?" he asked eagerly.

"Oh no, General. He will fight. He must. His honor requires it. He is a Miami! I regret that my arithmetic is not good. Eli taught me some, but I never went to the white man's school in Pennsylvania. He said I would not be welcomed there. I do think, however, that there will be more than two thousand warriors facing thee. The war chief Blue Jacket, who is a white man, will lead more than just his Shawnees. There will also be Potawatomi, Ojibwas, Soo Fox, some Iroquois, and a few British and French Canadians disguised as Indians.

"Why would they wish to disguise themselves in this way?" Sean asked.

Wayne answered the question. "The British have been given instructions to do nothing that might start another war with the Americans. In fact I have identical orders from President Washington! Please continue, Bluefoot."

"Thy cannon, although greatly feared by most Indians, would be of no use against the warriors concealed behind the many huge fallen trees. Also, the cavalry would hardly be able to move among the tangled branches. Little Turtle's troops, and the others, are to wait until the horses are stopped by the downed trees, then shoot both horses and riders with bullets and arrows."

"Just as we suspected from our other scouts' reports. Now, a very important question for either one of you. Will the British or the Canadians supply cannon for the battle?"

Sean now spoke up for the first time. "I'm sorry General, but I don't feel I have anything to say that will be of help. I was sick and in pain in the hut of an Indian healer nearly the whole time. But once, as he was packing some awful concoction into my eye, one of their chiefs entered and they seemed real angry. Since I don't speak their language, of course I did not understand, but they hardly sounded like persons anxious for the coming battle."

"Thank you," Wayne responded. He seemed reluctant to look at the heavy bandages encircling the private's face. "It is a terrible thing to lose an eye," he thought, "especially to someone as young as Private

O'Casey here."

"General Wayne," Tom said, standing and coming to attention, "I ask your pardon for allowing me, a mere scout, to offer a bit of advice. It is my opinion that you will not win this battle!"

For the first time in a long time a slight smile lightened the general's countenance. "And why do you say that, Tom Bluefoot?"

Having begun this ridiculous and possibly dangerous course of action, Tom stood resolutely and continued. "Because sir, you have not seen the cover that my people will have. The trees are uprooted and tangled together everywhere. The warriors will be well hidden, and can take their time loading and shooting at your soldiers, who may turn and run. Also, the Indians are very anxious to fight! I have seen them at the scalp dance! Should your infantry troops enter the fallen trees they will be no match for the furious Indians' tomahawks. And every brave, from his youth, has learned to shoot perhaps ten arrows in the time it takes for a soldier to load and fire one shot from his gun! And . . . your cavalry will be stopped by a line of logs the Indians have rolled into place several paces ahead of the windfalls!"

"Orderly!"

"Yes General?"

"Have Major Compton, Cavalry Commander, report to me at once!"

"Sir!"

Wayne was no longer smiling. "Your information may have been more helpful than you could know! You are ordered to stay within the sound of my voice tomorrow, no matter how the battle goes. Dismissed."

Even though he was a long way off, Caswell's bellows could be plainly heard. Having no specific orders for the rest of the day, Tom and Sean headed toward the grove of trees where the newly promoted Sergeant Caswell was giving his men some pointers.

"Get yer elbow up, man! Up!" The big man was in his element now, finally in charge! "Now you there. Why are you dropping onto one knee? You gonna have time for that tomorrow? Do yer shootin' standing up, then drop clear down, clear down, and reload. If any of youuns' rifles is like mine they got a real hair trigger on 'em. So don't pull your set trigger till you got a redskin plumb in yer sights." Cas pretended not to notice the growing number of recruits watching him, Tom and Sean among them.

"Tom," Sean finally said, "I got to lie down for a while. The whole side of my head feels like it's gonna explode! A headache sure ain't the word for it. I'm feeling sick to my stomach too. I'm going over to the surgeon's tent. Maybe he will give me a couple drops of that medicine he talked about. Lauderwin? Or lowdermin? Something like that. I'll try to see you tomorrow morning, but I doubt if I'll be well enough to be in the battle."

"You go ahead Sean. Don't even think about tomorrow. The

General said it right; you've already given more than your share to the army. We'll meet up as soon as we can, probably after the battle. If we win it!"

On the far side of the drill field, seventeen of the finest thoroughbreds in the cavalry were milling about, their mounts cursing at the confusion.

A large log had been dragged into place. One by one, the animals were urged into a gallop and forced to jump the log. All but two cleared the obstruction with several inches to spare. A great shout of laughter erupted when one of the two unsuccessful horses planted its feet just before reaching the log. The rider, sailing through the air, cleared the obstruction, but without his horse! He landed in a heap, growling curses.

The fifteen mounts which had successfully made the jump would, on General Wayne's orders, make up the only rank of cavalry to charge the fallen trees on the following day.

* * *

"Laudanum again is it? That's what they all want. I told you already I'd probably not have enough for the wounded soldiers. What makes you think I should give you any? You already had some last night."

"It's this awful headache, Captain. My eye hurts terrible, or at least it hurts where my eye used to be. I need some of that stuff real bad, doctor!"

The surgeon continued wiping his instruments clean with a dirty rag. A bone saw and an eight inch steel probe got special attention. When most of the crusted blood and rust was polished away he placed each instrument in order on a small stand. Two devices he even dunked in the bucket of water under his operating table. He continued his work, still ignoring his guest.

Sean gripped his head in both hands. "Please doctor, please! I've got to have that stuff or I think I'll go crazy!"

"You think you need it worse than some shot-up or tomahawked soldier is going to?" he growled. "What are your orders, private? Why are you bothering me with your complaints?"

"I guess I don't have any orders sir, at least none I'm aware of. I think the officers figured I'd be no good in the fighting. They were sure right about that! I'm sort of sick to my stomach too. What about that medicine, Captain?"

"No orders, eh? Tell you what. I'll give you five drops of laudanum. That'll see you through the night and maybe the next day. In return you can be my assistant during the battle. How does that sound to you?"

"How about ten of them drops?" Sean wheedled.

"Eight or none," the doctor growled. He measured the narcotic carefully, then dripped the bitter, brown liquid one drop at a time onto Sean's tongue. "They'll start to work in an hour or so. Lie down there and relax."

"I sure thank you Captain," Sean said, moving to a cot. "Of course I'd help you but I've only got one eye."

"I'm aware of that," the Captain said dryly. "But you won't need two eyes to hold a screaming man down while I saw off his leg!"

"I think you're trying to get me ready for what I'm going to be seeing tomorrow."

The surgeon opened the flap on his surgical tent. For a long moment he simply stared out at the sunset. When he turned back, Sean almost thought he was looking at a different person. The man seemed to have aged ten years in a minute! The doctor sat down wearily on the other cot. Without looking at Sean, he murmured, "believe me son, nothing, absolutely nothing I can tell you will prepare you for the horror of what can happen to a human body in war! You go to sleep now. Come morning, what you'll be doing will make you wish you'd saved that laudanum for then!"

"Wal, wal! How's old one-eye doin? Haw haw!" Big Cas and Tom Bluefoot had entered the surgeon's tent without even announcing themselves. As a brand new sergeant, Caswell was what the cavalry called "feeling his oats".

"If you're here to see Private O'Casey, you'd better hurry. He'll be nodding off before long. I gave him a few grains of laudanum a while ago."

"Sir," Caswell began politely, "I wouldn't be here, but the cavalry officer ordered me to come. He was watching me train our sharpshooters and said he seen my wounds startin' to bleed again. So here I be!"

"Let me see." The captain lifted Caswell's shirt. Sure enough both the entry and exit paths of the bullet were oozing blood. "Did you keep pulling the rolled bandage back and forth through the wound like I told you?" the doctor demanded.

"Well Captain, it's like this here," Cas began lamely, "I done that a time or two but it hurt like thunder. So I says to myself, Cas, I says, it might be better ifn I was to just . . ."

"So it hurt did it?" the doctor thundered. "Get hold of that tent post. I'm going to show you what really hurts!" The surgeon set himself and got a good grip on one end of the bandage protruding from Sergeant Caswell's side. He gave a quick, hard jerk. About half of the roll popped out of the bloody fissure, but some remained, out of sight. Disgustedly he pulled out the other protruding end.

Cas' normally ruddy face went chalk white. He hung onto the tent support and took several gasping breaths. "Yes sir!" He croaked. "That there hurt like the very old nick hisself!"

"There's a piece of muslin still in you, soldier. I can probe for it, or we can just leave it in there. What do you want me to do?"

"Leave it doc! Leave it!" Cas stumbled from the tent, needing some air!

Sergeant Caswell, by his own admission was a liar, a braggart, and a bully, but a man of greater courage and dedication to the army would be hard to find!

Tom and Sean left the tent, following the sergeant, but the doctor called them back. "Take that bucket and get me some fresh water from the creek before that laudanum begins to take effect. And while you're there wash out what's left of your big friend's bandage. Ring it out real good. We're going to need all the dressings we've got, and more. Hang it on the tent rope to dry. Might as well get some work out of you before you fall down! Go on now."

Back from the creek, Sean slid the dripping bucket under the table. The Captain was busy treating a corporal's foot, which appeared to be badly infected. "Did you have blisters son?" he asked as he worked.

"Yes sir. They were bad but I kept marching just the same. My boots were a little too big, so my foot kept slipping around in there. So I got blisters."

"Why didn't you request better fitting boots if you knew your foot was getting blisters?"

"I did, sir, but they said there weren't any more, no matter what size I needed. 'Be glad you got any!' the quartermaster said. 'We marched barefoot at Valley Forge in the dead of winter!' When he said that, I quit complaining and just marched on my blisters."

"Did you put powder in your boots?"

"I asked, but they said they didn't have anymore."

"If they didn't have powder to give, you should have made some."

"Make it you say? How in the world could I do that?"

The surgeon continued with his work, but replied, "Get some fine wood ashes. Hardwood ashes are best. Build up your fire on some flat rocks and let it burn clear down. Overnight is best. Scrape up the ashes, put some in your boots and a little right in your socks. It will help. I'd give you some foot powder, but I don't have any left either."

"What's that Irishman doing here? Isn't he the one who got whipped for helping a deserter or something?" the corporal asked, giving Sean a critical look. "Ow! What did you jab my sore foot like that for?"

"I did it so every time you take a step you'll remember that we're all just soldiers in General Wayne's army. Not Irish, not English, not German, not Indian. It so happens that this man and the scout he helped and got whipped for, might be considered heroes! They sneaked right into the enemy camp and got important information for the General! Now get out of here and mind what I said!"

Sean was astonished. He had no idea that anyone except General Wayne even knew about their mission, but as is true in every army, the word had spread! "Thank you for the kind words, Captain," Sean said. "But why do so many people hate us Irishmen?"

"A lot of reasons, son, but mostly because somebody taught them to! Now you better sit before you fall down. You look a little sleepy."

Sean grinned a little. "It don't hurt bad at all now Sir, thanks to that medicine you gave me."

"Before you fall asleep I have a question or two. Are you awake enough to answer?"

"I am now, but I don't know for how much longer. What did you want to ask me?"

With no more patients waiting outside, the doctor sat on the other cot and faced the young private. "Your friends told me you were very sick when you entered the Indian camp. Is that correct?"

"I surely was! I had such a high fever it felt like I was on fire!"

"I understand that you were taken to a native medicine man for treatment. You must have made a remarkable recovery. Do you remember what the healer gave you?"

"I was mighty sick, but I was able to see what he was going to do to me."

"Did he give you something to ingest?"

"What's 'ingest'?"

"Did you have to eat anything?"

"No Sir, but he made me drink a lot of really bitter-tasting stuff!"

"I don't suppose you know what it was, do you?"

"Yes sir, I do. He shredded up some leaves and dropped them into boiling water. I had to drink the stuff while it was still so hot it burned my tongue."

"Could you tell what kind of leaves they were? Maybe you were too sick."

"Oh no, Captain. He called them some kind of Indian name, but they were just leaves off a flowering dogwood. We had lots of those kinds of trees back home. In a couple hours I started to sweat a lot and the fever just plain left!"

"Well, well. What a story! The next time you see some of that dogwood, get me a sack full of the leaves, will you?"

"You bet Captain," Sean said, a sort of silly, lopsided grin on his face.

Big Cas and Tom reentered the tent. Each gave Sean a searching look.

"Lookee there, Bluefoot," Caswell said, pointing toward the marching men. He had recovered somewhat, but fresh blood was evident on his shirt. "Them's my boys over yonder. See them feathers sticking outn their hats? All of us sharpshooters gots them to wear in the battle. They're eagle feathers! Here's mine." He pulled a long white quill from his jacket.

"Won't that make your men better targets for the Indians to

shoot at? Where'd you get those feathers, Cas?"

"That old half-breed who's allus hangin' around camp sold them to me fer a pint of whiskey. He wanted a full jug, but I haggled him down."

Tom grinned but made no reply. They looked ridiculous, sticking straight up from the shooters' caps. He knew they were certainly not from any eagle! "Where'd you get the whiskey, Cas?" he asked.

"What whiskey?"

"The whiskey you traded for the feathers," Tom replied.

"Why I stold it, o'course. I got ways! Say Bluefoot, you notice I never calls you 'Stinkfoot' anymore?"

"I've noticed," Tom replied dryly. "And you ain't tried to kill me lately either."

"I ain't have I? Haw haw! Well Bluefoot since the fightin' begins soon I want to say that you ain't a bad sort of a guy, even if you are a redskin. I reckon there's a few of your kind that are almost o.k. I never said much about it but you shore saved me and the redhead back there on the trail outside of the Injuns' camps. Then you used your old noggin to get in and out of that mess with some good information for the General."

Tom was shocked. Big Cas had never spoken to him like this before. Haltingly, he began. "Well I need to tell you again how lucky I was that your rifle shot saved me. And I should have been scouting out ahead of the three of us on the way back. Maybe I could have kept you from getting shot."

"Shore enough pardner. I'd say we're about even up far as helping each other out is concerned. Before I go back to my men [he emphasized those last two words proudly] there's one more thing I got to get offn my chest."

Tom said nothing, but he noticed Cas' bloody hand pressed against the entry wound in his side. "What's that Cas?"

"You know I ain't one to think the worst on things, but for the first time in my worthless life I got a feeling that maybe it could go bad for me tomorrow. Now Bluefoot, I'm gonna ask you something and you'll oblige me with a straight answer. That one you killed in the Injuns' camp a couple years ago, the one where you had to run for it, that there one was a little girl, wasn't she?"

Tom was aghast. Had Caswell figured the whole thing out? Was the big man about to avenge the death of his little sister? He began to edge away, ready to run for his life once again.

"Come back here, you!" Cas growled. "I've had this figured for a long time. I ain't mad at you. I know you risked your own scalp to save that little one from what them screamin' devils would have done to her at the stake! I'm sayin' thankee fer what you done!" He extended his clean hand. Tom took it and winced at the power of the handshake.

"You'll be fine tomorrow, Cas. Your men need you leading them.

After the battle, if we win it, you'd better get the surgeon to probe for that piece of rag in your side. Seems to me that it ought to come out."

"I reckon you're right. I'll see to it tomorrow as soon as the sawbones can get to me."

Both a little embarrassed the big soldier and the skinny Wyandot scout went their separate ways, not looking back.

Sean slept peacefully, a beautiful smile on his face.

*   *   *

The camp was especially quiet that evening, as the men tried to get a little sleep on the night before the battle.

"'Cause I was there, that's why! Most of youuns wasn't even borned yet when me and the real soldiers was fighting the Revolution War. I'm telling you it was my idea to get General Washington to hire that there old Prussian. Baron Von-somethin-or-other his name was. He was a tough old bird, that there Prussian was. But he shorely whipped us into shape! Yes sir, he did for sure back there at Valley Forge."

Private Mapes shook his head in exasperation. "Here he goes again," he muttered to his tent mates. "That old man is the biggest liar in this man's army! If he ever even saw Washington it would be a surprise to me! If I wasn't so hungry I'd just stick a sock in his mouth, but his yarns do help take my mind off my growling belly 'cause of the rations we ain't been getting. So," he continued, "you just walked up to the Commanding General there in winter quarters, and started telling him how to fight the war, did you?" he asked sardonically.

"No I never! The General sent for me! See Washington and me growed up together, him and me did. So he knowed I had a head on me for the best ways of getting troops in line. The reason I suggested that he get that there Prussian fella was that . . ."

"For Pete's sake, Gimpy, will you shut your trap long enough for me to get a little sleep? I swear you are the talkinist man I ever knew!"

"Aw let him talk," one of the soldiers laughed. "He's better than a medicine show! Tell us what it was like during that winter, why don't you? And just leave out the part about how you won the war singlehanded."

Travis' whole demeanor seemed to change in an instant. It got very quiet around the small, smoky fire they'd built to discourage the mosquitos. For the first time in weeks the soldiers were really listening.

"I'll tell you boys there ain't never been anything like it. Cold? You don't have no idea about cold! Lookee here." He sat back, pulled off a dirty sock and thrust his foot forward. One of the recruits whistled in surprise. "See there? I ain't got but two toes on that there right foot. The others got froze off. You calls me 'Gimpy', well I guess you'd go gimping along too if you had something like that to walk on. Just try kicking a clod of dirt with toes like that. You'd see all right!"

"What happened to your toes after they got frozen?"

Private Mapes asked, politely enough.

"They turned black a-course. Heck's fire, I wasn't the only one losing body parts. Everybody knew them black ones had to come off. A sergeant said he'd do it for me and so I just let him. He took quite a while getting' his knife real sharp, and then he just up and done it! It didn't hurt too bad 'cause he was quick. He claimed he had taken off a bunch of other ones. What really hurt was when he got a old spoon red hot and just seared the places where them toes had been. That made me holler!"

No one said anything for a while. There was no way the old man could lie about his missing toes! "They say you Revolutionary soldiers were about starving during that winter. Is that true, Gimpy?"

"Huh! Hungry? Why youuns don't know nothing about hungry. Skaggs there was bellyachin' about thin rations. Well, sonny boy, when you get hungry enough to boil your shoe tongues and eat 'em, then you can tell me how hungry you are! Huh!" He pulled his sock back on, doing his best to fold it back over the gap.

"I heard they even made you men march and drill that winter. How could you do it, freezing and half starved like I've been told? That's pretty hard to believe."

"I don't care if you believe it or not! I wish somebody would have painted a picture of that so-called 'parade ground'. So many of us had falling apart shoes or no shoes at all, that the snow was more red than white. The Prussian General paid no attention to any fool dumb enough to complain. Or he'd use that swagger stick he allus carried to give them a few licks to shut 'em up. Still and all we learned to march, and right smart too!"

"Now I got one more thing to say before I get in my bedroll. I seen you boys grinning at my stories. Well I'm gonna tell you the truth right now. I did know George Washington when we was both just little sprouts. My pappy share-cropped for George's pa. Every once in a while, here he'd come. George I mean, riding a sorrel mare so big the youngun must have had to get on a stump to mount up. Talk about a rider! He couldn't have been more than five or six year old when he'd ride down there to our cabin, but already he could just make that horse do anything he wanted it to. Yes sir, he could ride! I didn't have no horse, us being about as poor as church mice, but that youngun would pull me up behind him and off we'd go. Like to skeered me to death he did. There wasn't a log or a bush he wouldn't have to jump over. I'd be hanging onto him tighter than a tick on a hound dog's rump. They was fun days back then."

"Since I ain't had nearly enough punishment for one day," Mapes said with a grin, "go ahead and tell us how it was you who suggested that George get General von Steuben to take charge of the troops."

"Shore! Shore! It was quite a coincerdenst how that come to be. See, my second cousin, Burl Bacon, was working the docks in Boston harbor when he seen that old Prussian officer come ashore.

Burl wasn't never nobody to hold back, so he just takes von Steuben to a saloon and buys him a drink. The long and short of it was when Burl told me all about this 'old country' soldier, I just goes right to Georgie and tells him he better get that man in his army before the British does!"

The laughter was loud and long. Growling bellies were forgotten as they enjoyed Gimpy's latest audacious yarn.

"What's so funny, soldiers?" The men scrambled to come to attention and salute General Wayne's Second in Command. Gimpy was the last man up, his arthritic knees popping audibly.

"Wal General Scott, sir, I was just telling them how me and my cousin Burl had . . ."

"Good heavens!" Scott exclaimed. "Is that you Sergeant Porter? General Wayne was just talking about you last week. What are you doing here man?"

"Sir it's just like this. After we whipped the Redcoats at Monmouth I headed home. Ma and Granma needed help getting the corn and wheat planted. When I heard that Wayne, I mean General Wayne, was to be ramroddin' this here sorry bunch, I just ups and re-joins."

"You come with me right now, Porter. The General will want to see you."

"Beggin' your pardon sir, but let's just let that go till after the battle tomorrow. I better stay close to these friends of mine to make sure they don't shoot theirselves in the foot!"

Still standing at attention, mouths open and eyes bugging, Gimpy's tent-mates looked for all the world like a family of scared screech owls!

*   *   *

As ordered, Tom Bluefoot did his best to stay within hearing of General Wayne's voice. It was not easy! Resplendent in his high-collared blue-grey coat and snug breeches, the big man was everywhere at once. His movements were not haphazard however. Subordinates followed, asking questions, taking orders, then hurrying away. Tom wondered why the General had spent so much critical time and attention to his immaculate uniform, complete with cocked hat and white neck scarf. But Wayne knew his business. Soldiers were in many ways much like children. They needed an imposing figure leading them. Wayne's impressive appearance on the field of battle adequately fulfilled that need!

The first ranks of foot soldiers were formed up, waiting for their orders. After a final flurry of activity, General Anthony Wayne mounted up and walked his horse calmly to the front. His sore foot was again causing much pain. With some effective needle work, a camp follower had let out, then re-sewed the seam in his uniform breeches, effectively hiding the wrappings underneath.

"Soldiers," he began in a voice that echoed off the surrounding forest, "today we will discover who among us has true courage. We will see those who follow the orders of their officers. Today I, your Commanding Officer, will know if nearly two years of rigorous discipline will result in ultimate total victory! I have been ruthless. Some might even call my methods cruel. Believe me I know the need. I am proud, very proud of each and every one of you, officers and non-coms as well. Gentlemen the field is yours. Do your duty. Have courage. Be brave. May God be with us all!"

The shout became a roar as every single soldier cheered his commander's address. The man they had hated, feared, and often doubted, was after all their General! They forgot the constant marching, the bad food, the floggings, and the arrogance. For him they would fight and if necessary die on this rainy morning near the mouth of the Maumee River.

Tom had cheered with the rest. Not feeling confident on horseback he remained on foot. He had correctly assumed that he would be able to stay near General Wayne, even if at times he might need to run. So far he had been largely ignored by the officers, so he stayed in the background, watching everything.

Thrum. Thrum. Thrum, thrum thrum thrum. The drummers began the cadence and the first rank of infantry marched forward. They were eager to engage the enemy, which remained out of sight behind the barricade of intertwined trunks and branches. The scene on that August morning was deceptively serene. The rain had stopped and the sun was shining. Already the men were sweating under their heavy uniforms, but characteristically, Wayne had expressly forbidden the removal of any item of clothing.

The Kentucky militia, a late addition to the two thousand five hundred man army, advanced confidently toward the concealed enemy. Suddenly the peaceful morning was shattered by the roar of muskets and the screams of the Indians' war cries. The Indians had fired first! Confused and disorganized, the newest troops turned and fled! Wayne and several other officers spurred their mounts into the midst of those in retreat. Roaring threats and curses they charged the runners, effectively slowing the rout enough for the regular infantry, with fixed bayonets, to march past and through them.

Not yet close enough to open fire, the regulars were suddenly shocked by a squad of fifteen or twenty men trotting resolutely forward, well out in front of them.

"Stand back, you cowards! This here's what we come for!" Tom, doing his best to stay near the General, had to smile. There was no question who was doing the yelling. "Fire at will, men!" Big Cas bellowed. He stopped running, raised his rifle, and took careful aim. He fired, but Tom could not see if the bullet had found its mark. Knowing Cas' marksmanship he was sure that it had!

The other members of the Sharpshooter Squad began firing. As they had been hurriedly taught, after each shot they dropped to the ground to reload. Caswell, Tom noticed had much trouble regaining his feet, but once erect his rifle remained steady for the shot. This time Tom plainly saw a warrior, perhaps anxious to prove his courage and "count coup" on the enemy, pitched forward in death.

Tom saw it then; a spreading stain on Sergeant Caswell's shirt. Whether it was from his previous wound or not, Tom could not tell. After firing and dropping to reload once more the big man made no effort to stand. He continued firing, and kneeling on one knee, motioned the squad forward ahead of him.

There was much confusion among the defenders. These soldiers of the Mad General were not firing in volleys as the Indians had been told to expect. Out in front were just a few men with some sort of ridiculous-looking white feathers in their caps. Trying to shoot at them was futile because they were out of musket range. Demonstrating heartbreaking courage, several Indians left their concealment and charged, attempting to get close enough to shoot at the marksmen. Not a one made it, but Pus-sic-sem-a, "Corn Saver", a noted and much-loved Ottawa sub-chief, got a shot off before he fell.

Sergeant Will Caswell, Sharpshooter Squad leader, braggart, bully, liar, and patriot, fell backward, shot through the neck. The white feather remained on his cap as it rolled away.

Many of the Indians still feeling safe behind their formidable natural barricade, continued to fight. Some had abandoned their muskets in favor of the bow. It was then that they were astonished by a sight they could hardly believe. Charging toward them at full gallop came a line of cavalry. Rather than pull up and dismount at the first barrier as the Indians expected, they came soaring up and over the tree trunks in a series of magnificent jumps. Once over this first obstacle their sabers were flashing as the panicked defenders were cut down almost at will. True, several horses were shot, one with arrows, and one had impaled itself on a broken branch. Four riders were killed when forced to dismount within the tangle.

At this critical juncture in the battle, Mad Anthony Wayne's much criticized strategy came into play. Rank upon rank of infantry marched forward, firing as they came. Bayonets flashing in the morning sun, they came, and came, and came! Of all the Shemanese weapons, the Indians most feared the bayonet, which they called "the long knives". Now these thin slivers of polished steel looked them in their very faces! The urge to turn and run was nearly impossible to overcome!

Even the bravest and most resourceful Indians began to realize that the battle was already lost to them. Those who were able dragged dead or wounded comrades back from the fray. Many bodies were left.

The main cavalry regiment had found little resistance as they charged across the open ground Tom had described west of the fallen timbers. Using sabers and pistols, they created a panic much like the fighting still going on within the downed trees. All the Indians who were able joined their fellow braves and fled north, heading for what they thought would be sanctuary in the British fort.

General Wayne called for a cease fire in order to avoid further slaughter of the retreating Indians. Toom-She-chi-Kwa, now having no trouble staying near the General, was surprised to hear his name called.

"Tom Twofoot," Major Blaski shouted. "Report to General Wayne immediately!" Smiling at the wrong name, Tom ran to the General's side. The big man had lost his hat, but other than that his uniform remained unblemished.

"My thanks to you will be expressed formally at a later time, Tom Bluefoot. Your scouting reports saved many lives and may even have helped in our speedy victory. Now however, find a mount and prepare a flag of truce. I must parlay with the British Commander at the fort. Meet me near the fort in one hour. Do not be late!"

Tom must now prepare himself for a sad duty. He had seen Sergeant Caswell fall, so had no trouble locating the body. He knelt beside the man he had once hated, but did not seek a pulse. Cas was obviously dead. Tom looked about for the rifle Caswell had been so proud of and so effective in its use. It was gone, probably taken by an Indian scavenging during the cease fire. The hat with its white feather was missing as well.

The surgeon's wagon was in plain sight not far to the rear. Tom hurried over. Wounded men were laid out in rows behind the wagon. The surgeon was busily moving among them, Sean O'Casey following him. "Sean! Sean. It's me, Tom. Are you o.k.? Cal got killed. He's lying right over there. Captain," Tom yelled, "can you take a look at my friend, Sergeant Caswell? Remember him? He's the big man who . . ."

"Is he dead?" the surgeon bellowed.

"Yes sir. I'm sure he is, but . . ."

"Then get out of the way. We're working with them as can still be helped!" He hurried away to examine the next man.

"Maybe you could help too," Sean yelled.

"Can't. Got to go with the General. I'll find you later."

*   *   *

"You're a real cutie!" the woman said, scrubbing the dried blood off her arms. "I always did like a red-headed man. What happened to your eye anyway?"

Sean rose from the creek bank, wiping his dripping hands on his trousers. The doctor, Captain Friederich Gruber, had allowed them a few minutes' rest before needing their help during the next surgery. "Lost my eye because of a flogging," Sean replied shortly.

"A flogging?" the camp follower cried. "That sergeant they always get to do the whipping was the one who did it, did he? That man's a butcher! How 'd he manage to get you in the face like that anyway?"

Embarrassed, Sean looked away. "I guess it wasn't really his fault. General Wayne ordered him to cut me across the face to mark me."

"What in the world did you do Sean to make the General order that?"

"It may have saved my life, 'cause I was to pretend to be a

deserter. That way I could go into the Indians' camps as a spy. When they saw my eye and everything they would sure see why I left the army to join up with them."

"That's long enough!" Captain Gruber shouted. "I need you two right now. Get back here!"

"Well here we go again, Sean," Mamie sighed as they hurried back.

The surgical tent had been set up next to the command station. Anyone within a hundred yards of it could hear the moans and cries of the wounded. The four most serious cases were lying on cots inside, some twenty others lined up on the ground. They lay under a sheet of canvas arranged to keep out the sun.

"What's your name son?" Gruber demanded roughly. "Didn't have sense enough to duck, eh?"

"Grafton," the soldier managed to reply through gritted teeth. His shattered arm was propped up on the cutting table.

"Are you Irish?" Sean asked, applying a tourniquet above the dripping wound.

"I am, sure enough. Are you?" he gasped, turning his head to see the surgeon's helper.

"That I am! That I am." Sean replied, laying on a thick Irish brogue. "My people came over here in sixty-nine from County Cork. Where did you live over there?"

The soldier seemed a little more relaxed. They talked about the Old Country some more. The surgeon was ready, but Sean motioned him back a step. "Now you know that your arm has to come off don't you?" Sean asked, patting the soldier on the leg. "If it don't come off you're gonna die for sure. Now us Irishmen can take it can't we?"

"Sure and Begorra we can!" the man grunted. "Do what ye have to do."

"First we're going to give you some strong pain killer. That will help a lot. Lean back and open your mouth."

Gruber shook his head and motioned angrily at the empty bottle of laudanum.

Sean gave the Captain an exaggerated wink and picked up a tin cup of coffee grounds.

"Swallow this mixture as quick as you can. Then Mamie's going to count to twenty-five real slow. Then this medicine will start to take effect. It's powerful stuff!"

Gruber shook his head in exasperation, but he waited while the woman slowly tolled the numbers.

"Now you just relax, private," Sean said. He and Mamie leaned over the man, pinning his arms, legs, and one good arm. Sean nodded to the surgeon and the operation began. It was over in four minutes, the soldier in a dead faint.

Mamie wrapped bandages as fast as she could.

Dr. Friederich Gruber spent a long moment staring quizzically at his one-eyed helper. "That was the easiest amputation I've done today," he growled. "What do you plan to do when your enlistment's over, young man?" he asked, rinsing his instruments in the bucket.

"I don't know yet. Guess I've got about another year of enlistment to go, so I won't need to decide for a while," he laughed.

"Well I'm a man who makes up his mind real quick. This is going to be my last year in the army. I plan to set up my own practice back in Pittsburgh where some of my relatives are. I think you could be a surgeon. You have a gift, son. I've seen it! When your enlistment's done come to Pittsburgh and look me up. I'll help you get your medical license. You can finish the training in about eight months. If you want, you can work with me for a while till you learn which end is the knife!" Without another word he ordered Sean and Mamie to bring in the next patient.

Sean was so surprised he nearly tripped over a tent peg. "Me a doctor?" he said to Mamie. "Maybe I'll do it!"

* * *

General Wayne had regained his hat. His clothes had been carefully brushed and his horse curried until she glistened in the afternoon sun. All the officers rested their horses in a bit of shade a hundred yards from fort Miami. Talking quietly together, they completely ignored the armed British regulars watching from the walls.

Wayne remained quiet for a long moment, reflecting on the battle which had so recently been concluded. He cast an appreciative eye on the scout, Tom Bluefoot, who sat uneasily on a nondescript nag nearby.

The young Wyandot had, it might be said, already lived several lives in his twenty-two years. Born in an Indian village, his alcoholic father had "sold" him to a kindly Quaker widower. Six happy years in the white man's world had been suddenly interrupted by the unexpected return of his Wyandot father. Back among his forbears once more, he had been forced to run away. Having nowhere else to go, he had eventually joined the American army.

The General shook his head sadly as he considered the fact that he had then ordered Tom Bluefoot's return to the native villages as a spy. That the man had been successful, and had made it back with valuable information only added to the saga. Wayne however, knowing value where he saw it, would put the scout in danger once again!

"Tom Bluefoot," the General called, "come forward."

The scout kicked his aging mount into a trot. Not a trained horseman he simply hung onto the saddle horn and bounced along until he reached Wayne's side. In order to salute he had to let go of the saddle horn. He very nearly slid off the horse, but managed to catch himself in time.

Wayne and another officer smiled at the clumsy display, but the General began immediately. "You have the white flag I see," he began. Tom struggled with the unwieldy device until he could attempt to hand it over. "No, Private," Wayne said. "You will carry the white flag. You have told us that you are personally acquainted with both Chiefs Little Turtle and Blue Jacket. Is that the truth, Tom?"

"Sir! Yes sir. I know them well, although I have not spoken directly to Chief Blue Jacket. I also know Tenskwatawa, Tecumseh's brother, who is called 'The Prophet'. Unfortunately General, they also know me! They would like nothing better than to see me being slowly roasted to death at the stake!"

"Of course, Private. Fortunes of war! Before you dismount or fall off, look down at the south wall of the fort. Do you see the crowd of Indians standing there, still hoping to be let inside?"

"Yes sir, I see them. They were betrayed sir, just as Little Turtle expected. They were led to believe that if the battle did not go well they could take refuge behind the walls. Little Turtle never did trust the British, even though he seemed to be good friends with McKee."

"Take this," said the General. He handed Tom a beautiful three-sectioned telescope. "See if you can recognize any of the chiefs in that crowd. You'd better dismount first!" he added hastily.

Tom could hardly believe that he was being trusted with such a wonderful instrument. Unable to keep the heavy brass spyglass steady, he finally laid it over a low branch. The warriors seemed to leap toward him. "Aho!" he cried in wonder. He scanned the group carefully from one end to the other. For several minutes he continued to observe the mostly motionless, dejected Indians.

"Well?" General Wayne snapped. "What can you tell us?"

"Sorry General, but this thing is so . . .so wonderful that I forgot to report to thee!"

"I'm waiting, Private Bluefoot!" Wayne growled impatiently.

Tom finally handed the glass over. "Blue Jacket is there. I can pick him out easily. I think also 'The Prophet'. Two others appear to be chiefs but I don't know them. I also saw Roundhead, Chief of our Wyandots."

"And Little Turtle. Did you see him there?" Major Scott asked.

"I think so, but the braves kept moving. It was hard to be sure. Let me look again!" Tom said eagerly, reaching for the telescope.

"There is no more time to waste. I wish the parlay to begin before many more Indians begin to melt away into the forest. Take your flag of truce and mount up. There will be six of us." He motioned for the other officers he had chosen to come forward.

"I am to be with you and the other officers? Ride right by the warriors? Couldn't someone else carry the flag?" Tom asked, obviously frightened.

"Are you attempting to disobey my orders, Private?" General Wayne asked calmly, his eyes flashing fire.

"Oh no Sir! Not at all, General. But there are those standing at the wall of the fort who know me very well. They will shoot me with arrows or with a gun. They know now that I have been a spy who betrayed them. I will go if thou givest me a direct order, but I am sure that if I do, thou will quickly lose thy interpreter!" Fear and nervousness had once again brought back his Quaker speech patterns.

"Well put," said Wayne, surprising the others nearby. "Adjutant!" he called. "Summon Sergeant Caswell and five of his sharpshooters immediately."

"Sorry General, but I believe Sergeant Caswell did not survive the battle," the adjutant said.

"I see. That is too bad. He was a good soldier who, although badly wounded, did his duty. Bring the five sharpshooters anyway."

The small troop stopped less than fifty paces from the now unmoving warriors. Tom's flag moved slightly in the late afternoon breeze as Blue Jacket and two others stepped forward, boldly enough. One minor chief shouted angrily at Wayne and the rest of his entourage, giving Tom his first opportunity to interpret. "He asks why the white chiefs are accompanied by five soldiers armed with 'long shooter' rifle guns."

Wayne replied in his parade grounds voice, knowing that perhaps only Blue Jacket himself understood his words. He nodded for Toom-She-chi-Kwa to interpret. "My chief, General Mad Anthony Wayne, warns each and every Indian that if harm comes to any one of this group, including me [Tom added these two words to those of the

General] the long shooter guns will fire at every one of your chiefs. The battle is over! No vengeance will be tolerated!" The parlay continued for a short time without further incident.

The situation was tenuous to say the least. Both Major William Campbell, Commander of the British fort , and General Wayne had been strongly cautioned by their respective governments about allowing any hostilities which could lead to another British-American war. As the defeated and dejected Indians stood or sat against the log walls The American General forbade bringing the cannon forward. There was no need.

The British Commandant remained arrogant, secure behind the walls and backed up by several companies of red-coated, well-armed soldiers. The French and Canadians had slipped away, more afraid of retaliation by the betrayed Indians than they were of the Americans.

Tom found himself no longer needed as the interpreter. A series of notes had been shuttled back and forth between General Wayne and Major Campbell. Since both could read these well enough, Tom was dismissed for the rest of the evening.

The parlays would continue for two more days with little but blustering accomplished.

Before he left the General's side, Tom, still on foot, came to attention and addressed the victor. "Sir! Pardon the interruption General Wayne, but may I have a word with you?"

"You may but be quick."

"Some are saying that Major Covington and the Dragoons have been ordered to burn the remaining native villages and destroy any standing crops. As an Indian, a Wyandot, I know well what that will mean for the women and children when the winter snows arrive."

Two accompanying officers were astonished to see General Wayne slowly dismount, favoring his painful leg. "Come and sit with me," he said, limping to a shaded spot under a big maple tree. The others began to follow but the General waved them away. Seated with his bad leg extended, he turned to face the scout.

Tom was appalled at the weariness in the big man's face, but his uniform was still unblemished and his boots showed little dust. He offered Tom a drink from his canteen, but the younger man refused. Wiping his mouth with an immaculate handkerchief he began to speak.

"Do you think being in charge of a great army is an easy task?" he asked wearily. Without waiting for a reply he continued. "I am not unaware of the plight my orders will place upon your people. Especially those who have taken no part in this conflict. It is one thing to bring great harm to an enemy who is doing his best to kill you! It is quite another however to cause deliberate suffering to his wife and to his children." He raised the canteen again but this time did not offer it to the scout. It was almost as if he had forgotten that Tom was there.

"In the Revolution under General George Washington I had sent squads of men into situations that were almost certain to result in their deaths. Often it was to create a diversion or in some other way to aid in a major campaign. Was such action justified? Only God knows!" He turned to the young Indian again. "I need not expound further on this, for you and your two friends were ordered on such a mission yourselves not many days ago. Thankfully you survived. I sent you because I needed information that you might be able to provide. That you were successful and made your escape gave me great pleasure, as I have become fond of you. The floggings were at my orders as well. Whether you believe it or not, these punishments also were meant to save your lives when you entered the enemy camps."

"Thou hast done well, and only did what had to be done."

Wayne hardly heard. He began again. "The victory must be so completely ruthless that the chiefs will have no choice but to meet for a treaty of peace. They will, but I will tell you what will happen after all the treaties are signed." He took a long weary breath. "The chiefs will return to their people and in their councils explain the conditions agreed upon. Settlers will soon come in however, paying no attention to terms of the treaty, if they had even been told of them. They will build their cabins on land reserved for the natives. And so," he groaned miserably, "homes will be burned and people butchered in justifiable retaliation. Then the army will be asked to punish the Indians.
And on and on it goes! Report to me at noon tomorrow, Private Bluefoot. Dismissed." He limped away, calling to his subordinates.

A little light still silvered the treetops. Tom felt no fear as he mounted the nag and kicked her straight toward the fort. Most of the Indians were sitting down now, talking quietly in small groups. He dismounted awkwardly near the south wall. Doing his best to ignore the looks of hatred directed his way, he tied the old bay to a tree and walked purposefully toward a familiar figure leaning against the fort.

"Aho!" Bear said, loudly enough that many turned in their direction. "You are skinny and not very strong," old Bear remarked bluntly, "but you are a warrior worthy of some respect! I knew when we met on the trail that you were a clever and resourceful Wyandot. You fooled me completely. Would that you had remained with your own people and helped us fight! I have no bad feelings toward you at all. After all, you had some Shemanese thinking clouding up your head! What happened to the one-eyed soldier and the other one who is even bigger than me?"

Tom was so surprised and grateful he could hardly speak. Well he knew that his people admired cleverness and deceit above every other virtue, except for successful thievery! Bear's endorsement would do a great deal to help him be tolerated among the defeated braves eyeing them both. "The big man was killed this morning. The soldier who lost his eye to the soldiers' whip is helping the white doctor see to the wounded and dying. I am glad, Bear, that you hold no hatred for me. I am troubled in my spirit. It is as if two people are at war in my heart. One is red and one white."

"What will you do now, Toom-She-chi-Kwa?"

"I think the mad general wants me to act as one of the interpreters if a treaty of peace is arranged. Perhaps I can be of some help to our people if I am to do that duty. Nothing is certain for me at this time."

Bear stalked off, caring little what happened next.

* * *

"Toomie! Oha, Toomie, my son!" Tom was brought up short by the voice he would always recognize. Tottering toward him was the pathetic figure of the man who had sold him to the Quaker. Even though he had come for his son again six years later, it was still hard for Tom to think of this man as his real father.

"Aho, father. It is good to see you again. Are you well?"

"No! Oh no, I am not well. I am in great need, my son. I have no place to go. My legs fail me. I cannot hunt. My days are shameful, as only women's work is given to me. I help in the gardens. I clean up after the horses. I even help in scraping and tanning skins!"

"But father, you are a man still. Even if you cannot do the work of a man you should never take on the tasks of our sisters and mothers!" Tom felt a great surge of pity for this wreck which had once been a proud member of the Wyandot tribe, even in his younger years, a "keeper of the pipe"!

"My son, do you have any silver money? I am in great need!"

"No father. I have some of the soldier money. Not much. It is made of paper, not silver."

Tom's father made a pitiful face. "I'm hungry, Toomie. It is hard for me to get food. How I wish you could help me!"

"But surely your sister will see that you do not go hungry. My aunt is a kindly woman. She will share what she has with almost anyone. Why don't you go to her?"

"My sister, your aunt, has gone from here. She and many others left just before the battle. They said they would go to the west, where the white man would never go. I hope they are safe."

"Have you then no way to get food, father?" Tom asked.

"Ah but I do have one way. A small way." He opened the ragged "possibles bag" which hung from one shoulder. "Look in here." He rummaged around for a moment then found a tiny bow and arrow, no bigger than his hand. "And see this." Now he pulled out a miniature canoe made of slippery elm bark.

"What are these things?" Tom asked, puzzled.

"I sell them to the redcoats. They give them to their children. I get a farthing or two that way. Look at this." He pulled out a corn husk doll, complete with an acorn head. "See?" he said proudly.

Tom turned away and pretended to re-button his shirt. He could not bear to let his father see his tears.

*   *   *

During the next few weeks General Wayne ordered the army to bury the few dead, see to the wounded, and prepare to return to Fort Defiance for the winter. Despite Tom's eloquent plea, the Indian villages had been burned and all crops still standing fired as well. Wayne had given strict orders that no looting was to be tolerated. Still a few soldiers had risked a flogging to scavenge for souvenirs or usable items before the flames engulfed everything. Two who were caught disobeying this order received fifty lashes each. That effectively ended any further thievery!

Tom saw little of the General during that fall. He was only summoned when there was the infrequent need for an interpreter. Most of the defeated braves built temporary shelters in the vicinity of Fort Defiance, or established camps in the nearby forests. Some began rebuilding the burned out villages. There were no significant raids on American homesteaders, but some horse stealing still went on as occasions presented themselves. The General assigned various subordinates to deal with these problems, but in actuality little was done about them.

Several of the Indian scouts had left the army. No one seemed to care, as it was apparent that their considerable skills were no longer needed. Tom was about to seek permission to leave as well, when he was surprised by an order to meet with General Wayne.

Far from the usual cold and drafty tents that had been his headquarters, Wayne was established in a log house inside the fort. A fire was blazing in the fireplace, and the General was seated, boots off and stockinged feet extended toward the fire. He did not ask Tom to sit, mainly perhaps because there was only one crude chair and Wayne was in it! "Tom Bluefoot," he began, "have you yet been honored for your part in the battle at the fallen trees?"

"No General. But there is no need. I am only grateful that the fighting is over. That is reward enough."

"Well said! Well said. But I plan to yet honor you in some way. That is not, however, why you have been summoned here. I have another very important mission for you. One in which you can be of great service to your people and to this country as well." He stopped speaking but kept his eyes on the young Indian standing before him.

"I will do all I can, General," Tom said, careful not to commit to whatever was coming next.

"I know you will. This is how you can help. In the summer I plan to hold a grand counsel at the fort in Green Ville. It would be hard for me to describe the importance of this meeting. If successful, the very nature of white and Indian relations could be changed forever. My hope is that no more wars will be necessary between your people and mine. Can you see how critical the outcome of any treaty made there can be for future generations?"

"Perhaps," Tom said hesitantly.

"Perhaps?" Wayne replied angrily. "What do you mean by that, Tom Bluefoot?"

"I meant no disrespect General, but you know as well as I that treaties can be broken. Still I can see that the attempt must be made. But I cannot see how I can be of any real help in this endeavor."

Somewhat mollified, Wayne continued. "Of course. If the outcome has any chance of lasting success all tribes must be represented. In the past some treaties were poorly conceived and therefore doomed to failure. Those signing the agreements were often not even the chiefs with the authority to do so. This must not happen at Green Ville!"

"I agree, but I still cannot see how . . ."

The General interrupted impatiently. "I am preparing a six-man unit under Major Mark Comstos. Their job will be to travel wherever it takes, inviting and urging the principal chiefs of every tribe to attend the counsel. I wish for you to travel with them, not only as interpreter, but as a sort of advisor as well. I am not ordering this, but I am urgently asking. What do you say?"

Tom spoke up boldly. "Of course I will agree. Anything I can do to promote a lasting peace I will do. But there are problems."

"What problems, Private Bluefoot? You are still a member of the army. Therefore I can order you to go if that becomes necessary."

"Truly General Wayne I would not be welcome in many villages. I am known to them as a deserter and a traitor. Some would be happy to kill me on sight! Even though I did what I did to save lives, there would be few who would believe that."

"I understand but I also know you! From what I have observed and have been told, you have a cool head and a quick mind, which have saved you from various dangers before. I still wish for you to agree."

Tom was silent for a moment then spoke again. "I will go, but I ask a favor in return."

A real smile stretched across General Wayne's face. "And what might that be, Bluefoot?"

"It is about my father," Tom said quickly. "I would ask that he be included in the delegation."

"That could probably be arranged. Do you refer to the Quaker gentleman with whom you spent some years?"

"No, I speak of my real father. A Wyandot."

"Why should I grant this request?" The General was truly curious.

"Because he is sick. That is . . .well . . .I mean . . ."

"Speak up! What is the problem? If your father is sick why subject him to what will amount to months of rigorous travel?"

"The sickness is of strong drink! If I don't get him away from those who sell it to him I think he will die. Marching and being far from the 'devil water' may give him new life. At least I would like to try."

"You are a remarkable young man!" The General stated. "Your words convince me even more that you will do a great deal of good with our plans for the treaty at Green Ville! Your request is granted. Find your father and bring him here within two weeks, when the delegation will be ready to travel."

* * *

"Why are you here Toom-She-chi-Kwa? You are not wanted in this village. It is thanks to you that we continue searching through the ashes of what was once our villages! The soldiers of the Mad General did this to us, and one who knows tells us that <u>you helped them!</u> Do you know what I have found of value in all my searching? <u>Do you?"</u>

"I am sorry Sec-se-tep. You are right. I did help the white soldiers, but I did it because . . ."

"Four steel fishhooks."

"What did you say?"

"Four fishhooks, for which I had had to pay two fox pelts and a raccoon skin hat. That is all I found of value. Everything else from my wegiwa was either burned up or stolen. So . . .go away before someone shoots you with an arrow!"

"I am sorry," Tom doggedly repeated. "I am only here to search for my father. He is called 'Falls Down A Lot'. Do you know him?"

The older brave's face wrinkled in contempt. "Aho! I know him. Everyone knows him! He is not here. We drove him out of our village half a moon after the great battle. The Redcoats had forced him to move away from the fort so he came here. We were tired of his begging and crying. We are glad he is gone. Why do you want to find him? You are better off without that wreck of a man, father or not."

The angry diatribe had evidently caused the man to forget some of his accusations about Tom's disloyalty. Almost kindly, he said, "My grandmother took pity on him, claiming she knew him before he became a slave to the devil drink. She learned that he had gone to Detroit and was working as a skinner for some French trappers. This may be true. I can help you no more than this. Gitchie Manitou go with you."

Tom was fortunate. A French trader agreed to allow the young Indian to accompany him on his return trip to Detroit. They walked until they reached Lautraub's cached canoe, carefully hidden in the willows along the Maumee. It was then that Tom began to earn his way. Paddling was much harder than he could have imagined. Every night his arms and shoulders ached and throbbed. Still, traveling mostly by water, they reached Detroit in only a few days.

The Frenchman was of further service then. It happened that he knew where Tom's father was working, dressing and tanning hides.

"Aho! Toom-She-chi-Kwa! Is that really you? Have you any silver money, my son? I am very hungry. Why are you here? Have you come to chase away the *borgles?"*

"It is good to see you again, my father. I do not have any silver," he lied. "But I do have some food left. Can you leave your work long enough to eat with your son?"

"Pah! There is no longer any work for me. These two have brought no skins for three days. They say I do not do good work so they do not pay. All day I am hungry, and then at night . . . at night . . .the *borgles* come!"

"What is this you say?" Tom asked, alarmed. "What do you mean, *borgles?"*

"They come, Toomie! They come and I fear them! Sometimes they even come during the day. Snakes, wild beasts, fierce faces! Something like ants or beetles get under my skin and torment me. I think I am dying. I hope I am dying. Aho, Toomie! Can you help me? Can you?"

"Yes, I can help you. I have arranged for you to travel with me and some soldiers. Our mission is to visit all the major tribes and convince their chiefs to attend the great Council at Green Ville. You and I must be at Fort Defiance within a week. Can you walk far?"

"I can walk, but I am slow. Unless I have the white man's brown water I will not be able to walk at all! You must get some for me, my son. Get it soon, then we can walk."

"Where can I get the devil drink?" Tom asked. He did not intend to provide liquor to this man who was already practically ruined by it, but he also knew that they must be heading south soon. That very day!

"This way! This way!" Myteksic said, hobbling off through a collection of shacks.

"Get out!" the big man ordered. "Unless you pay I give you no whiskey, you know that. Who is that?"

Tom's father tried to look proud. "He is my son. He has silver money. We will buy one large jug. Hurry up!"

"A small jug!" Tom stated resolutely, counting out a few coins.

"You're going to need more liquor than that, Injun!" the owner of the trading post sneered. But he handed over the jug. Myteksic reached desperately for it, but Tom kept it under one arm. "You can have a little as soon as we reach Otter Creek. Not before!"

Tom had to smile a little at how soon they reached the designated creek, the first of what was to become many such goals. He had to forcefully grab the jug before his father could drink much. Tom wanted to get far enough south that there would be no further source of the strong drink. "When this is gone there may be trouble," he thought ruefully.

Using the liquor as incentive, at first they made good progress, but inevitably it was soon gone. Whining, pleading, threatening, Myteksic made life miserable for his son.

Tom had hoped to ration the whiskey carefully enough that it would see them all the way to Fort Defiance. He was unaware of how devious a drunk could be. In the middle of the third night, Myteksic awoke, thrashing about and screaming. "Get away! Go! Go down in the black water! Get away! Oh! Ah, oh!"

Tom shook the man savagely but it did no good. He continued to cry out, scrabbling sideways in the darkness. The rest of the night saw one crisis after another.

Dawn's light showed a young man exhausted and pale, his father a human wreck, hardly able to stand, let alone walk. "The borgles, Toomie Did you see them? They came just like I said. Oh Toomie, I need the brown drink. I must have it! I cannot endure another night like that. We must go back. Give me silver money for the trader. Then we can go on or journey again, I promise."

"It is thine own fault!" Tom raged. "I saw thee sneaking gulps of that stuff when thou thought I was not looking. Now it is all gone. I will fill the empty jug with water as soon as we come to a creek. Thou wilt have to drink only water from now on. Get up! We must be on the trail. General Wayne is expecting us." Tom was unaware that the stress of directing his addicted father had caused the recurrence of the Quaker language patterns.

"Give me money!" Myteksic shouted. "I go back to Detroit. Do not try to stop me. You go on. I do not want to go to the Indian villages with you and the soldiers. I never did!"

The old man struggled to his feet and grabbed for the empty jug. "Give me that, my son," he said, reaching for it. "I am your father. You will obey and do what I tell you. Give me the jug!"

Tom raised the vessel and flung it down on a rock, smashing it to pieces. He picked up a broken branch, and holding it in two hands backed several steps away. "Nothing would please me more that to obey my real father," he said calmly. "but thou art no longer anyone's father. Thou art a madman! Still I will see that thou go with the General's delegation. No more whiskey! It will be hard but I will help. We go!"

The man made a grab for the club, but stumbled and fell. Tom had to turn away in order to hide his tears, but he was resolute.

Finally they reached Fort Defiance, two days late. Fortunately the departure had been postponed, as some of the gifts the delegation was to take had not yet arrived. Tom could see some improvement in his father, but he knew it would be hard to keep him from somehow getting liquor at the fort.

* * *

Tom and his father led the way, riding double. The five uniformed soldiers and the officer, Major Compton, followed in single file, grateful for the Indian's ability to navigate the nearly invisible trails.

The travel was much easier now that the May sunshine had whisked away the snow, and dried up much of the mud. The flag of truce carried by a yellow-haired sergeant was hardly needed any longer. Word of the delegation's visits had sped rapidly ahead of them from village to village, so most of the time they were expected. Sometimes they were welcomed cordially, but more often the men were met with such hostility that the soldiers kept their muskets at port arms. Thankfully so far there had been no violence.

Toom-She-chi-Kwa, elated with the rapid improvement his father was making, showed his worth time after time. As the young scout solemnly explained to the gatherings the reason for the delegation, looks of anger and hostility usually changed to albeit reluctant agreement. Most were sick of warfare and what it had done to families as well as to their warriors. Many tribes, due to General Wayne's policies, were reduced to near starvation. Therefore when the Major's speeches, Tom interpreting as best he could, explained the payments to be distributed at the Grand Council, they listened eagerly.

One by one their route took them to the main villages of the Kickapoo, Wea, Chippewa, Ottawa, and the Delaware. Success had been remarkable. They were even honored by a few of the chiefs. But not by all!

Blue Jacket stood, arms folded and head thrown back. Tecumseh was not present, but his brother, The Prophet, was seated nearby. "What can you say that I might be persuaded to believe you? A white man, as I once was," Blue Jacket continued angrily, "can be trusted about as far as a porcupine can fly! You speak of all these gifts and even great amounts of English money that is to be given to us at the fort in Green Ville. I do not believe you! Whiskey! To be sure, that will be given. Then when all are confused and falling down, such as I often saw this man," he jabbed a long finger at Tom's father, "then the parlay will begin. We will be cheated once again. And why, if you expect the many chiefs to believe you, why do you tolerate the drunkard's son sent to interpret for you? That he is a traitor to his own people is well known by all. Pah!" His glare of rage was fastened upon Toom-She-chi-Kwa.

Wearily Tom did his best to assure the chief of the honesty that General Wayne was attempting to bring to the Council of Peace. When he finished, Blue Jacket astonished the delegation by stating the following:

"I will be at Green Ville in what you call the month of August. Furthermore I will consider signing the treaty in behalf of all the Shawnee. I will not, however, agree to any order to lay down our arms forever. I have not finished with the Shemanese, but I may soon have a 'present' for them! It will be one they will not enjoy!" With those words he left the lodge and was seen no more.

After this the parlays went well. Tarhe and Roundhead of the Wyandot, as well as chiefs of the Delaware, Potawatomie, and Kaskaskia agreed to attend. Furthermore they promised to spread the word to several other chiefs if for some reason they had not been contacted by General Wayne's emissaries.

Little Turtle's town was to be their last stop. All in all their journeys had met with resounding success. Certainly the promise of gifts and annuities to be awarded at the Grand Council had much to do with their agreement.

"Aho! The trickster returns!" Michikinikwa said, not unkindly. "And is this Falls Down A Lot? Is he not your father? He seems to be much improved. How has this been accomplished?"

Tom spoke respectfully to the Miami chief, telling briefly some of the struggles it had been to clean his father's system of the devil drink. Little Turtle nodded in agreement, but said no more about it. Myteksic held himself aloof, smiling with justifiable pride. Tom's expression echoed that of his proud father, grateful to have the man back to nearly what he had once been.

The parlay seemed to be proceeding very well, but both Tom and the Major had begun to notice a young brave standing just beyond the delegation, on his face a look of furious anger. A member of the Cat nation, also known as the Erie, First Hunter and others of his tribe had joined with the Miami when starvation had seemed eminent. Little Turtle, a man who missed very little, took a step toward the brave and made a motion of dismissal. All were astonished when an audible "click" proved that the angry man had drawn a musket from beneath his blanket. Suddenly he had it aimed directly at Tom Bluefoot's chest.

His voice low and menacing, he began to speak. "You are a great

Chief, Michikinikwa, but all can see that the Shemanese have bewitched you. Where is the warrior who led us against Harimar and the Saint of Clair? Where is he? I see before me only a man making plans to accept the gifts and worthless promises of the whites at the Green Ville fort!" Cutting his eyes to the left he glowered at Tom Bluefoot. "And you!" he snarled. "I know you. A traitor to our people! An accursed spy for the Mad General. And now you are back here once more, filling Michikinikwa's mind with even more lies. No one has seen fit to seek vengeance upon you. All were too weak and fearful but I am not! Move away from us. Now you will die!"

Tom's father leaped to his feet like a striking panther. One strong hand closed on the muzzle, pulling it away from his son. They struggled briefly as Little Turtle rushed toward them. The musket roared. Myteksic fell backward, the musket ball having struck him under the chin and exited his skull. He died a brave man, such as he had once been.

The soldiers grabbed the Erie and held him, but it was Little Turtle himself who killed him with one thrust of his knife.

* * *

Toom-She-chi-Kwa had mourned the father he hardly knew, but with little true grief. The burial ceremony, a hasty affair, had been attended by a few old men and women who had known the man in former years. His son paid homage according to the customs of the

Wyandot, but it was actually with some relief that he had set off for Green Ville to await the Grand Council.

"Glad to see you Sergeant Bluefoot," General Wayne had said at his return. "My condolences on the death of your father."

"Thou knew of Myteksic's death?" Tom asked, surprised. "And why did thee call me 'sergeant'? I actually have only a private's rating, sir."

"I was told the entire story by Little Turtle himself. I know you were apprehensive about your mission, and you nearly lost your life at the end of it. Your father must have been a brave man. The chief seems to hold no anger toward you, even though he is well aware of your activities as my agent among his people. He is a very intelligent man, and a crafty one as well! I would expect he will drive a hard bargain for his Miamis!"

"Begging your pardon sir, it's about my rank."

"Ah yes, I'm promoting you to sergeant. I do this partly because I feel we never did honor you for providing critical information before the battle." He scribbled a few words on a scrap of paper and handed it to Tom. "See the paymaster and collect your back wages. The quartermaster will supply you with a regulation sergeant's uniform."

"Sir, with due respect sir, I prefer to dress as the Wyandot that I am. If I am still to act as one of the interpreters during the Council, I think being in regular Indian clothing would lend credibility to my words, sir."

"Tom Bluefoot you are right of course! I can see that once again you will be of great service to your people and to mine. Dress as you see fit. I must admit that your buckskins will feel much cooler than army issue in this summer heat!" Wayne was silent for quite a while. Tom stood and waited.

"Thank you sir. Am I dismissed?"

"One more thing. What is the condition of your friend, the private who lost an eye?" Wayne looked a little sheepish as he asked the question.

"He is well. The surgeon tells everyone that Private O'Casey seems to have a true gift of healing. The Captain has offered to take him on as an apprentice surgeon when their enlistment times are up. I believe they plan to locate near Pittsburgh and set up private practice. I'll tell Sean that you asked about him. Thank you, General."

Wayne gave a sigh of genuine relief. "You may tell him more than that, Sergeant Bluefoot. Have him report to me tomorrow, as soon as he has a moment to spare from his duties as the surgeon's helper. I will issue written orders that he be permanently attached to Captain Friederich's medical unit. He can begin his apprenticeship immediately, while still in the army! Adjutant!"

"Sir!"

"Have the surgeon report to my office immediately."

Tom could hardly believe his eyes as he left the General's headquarters. Indian lodges had sprung up like mushrooms in nearly every clearing within sight of the fort. Resplendent in beads, feathers and silver, every Indian who could claim even the most remote designation as chief stalked importantly about, casting covetous glances at the wagons loaded with "presents". None had been distributed yet however. Squads of soldiers stood guard over the treasures night and day, making sure that thefts of the goods was not possible.

"Hey Injun, what happened to the big sergeant who led out on the sharpshooters? Did he talk some redskins to death? Haw haw!"

Calmly Tom turned toward the soldier. "You will speak with respect when you address me, private!" He said, pointing to the sergeant's stripes he had pinned to his tunic.

"What the . . . Where'd you get them stripes, Bluefoot? Stole 'em I reckon. You better not let the Lieutenant catch you with 'em. You'll feel the cat on your back for sure!"

"General Wayne himself promoted me, private," Tom replied, again emphasizing the loud-mouthed soldier's inferior rank, "and as for the Lieutenant, why don't thou ask him. He was there when I was promoted. Now I'll accept an apology for thy crude remarks about Sergeant Caswell. He entered the battle already wounded, conducted himself bravely, led his unit with honor, and was shot down by Indian gunfire. I'm waiting, private!"

"Uh . . .well I guess I'm a little sorry about what I said, Sergeant. I 'pologize shor enough. Meant no harm, I didn't, but . . .where'd you learn to talk English so good?"

"That will be all, soldier. In future watch thy mouth."

Tom stalked away, hiding a big grin behind one hand. "It's true!" he exalted. "Rank does have its privileges!"

Toom-she-chi-Kwa saw little of the General as the month of June was coming to an end. Several of the chiefs he had counseled with over the winter acknowledged him with a nod or a grunt. Some did not. It was a very brave, if not foolhardy thing that the General was doing. Hundreds, perhaps thousands of Indians were assembled there, many with only thinly disguised hatred on their faces. Most had not wanted to come, but as Tom and the major had so patiently explained, actually they had little choice. Only the anticipation of the distribution of gifts and the promise of continuing yearly annuities prevented possible bloodshed. Thankfully, the gathering remained peaceful, at least on the surface.

In mid-July Tom was summoned to General Wayne's headquarters. Waiting to be addressed, the young Indian sergeant had time to observe the demeanor of the other officers assembled there. Not a one seemed pleased to see him, and several exhibited expressions of anger or disgust. Tom could well imagine what they were thinking. "Why is our General taking time to talk with an Indian? Wayne has always made up his own mind, and he usually does it quick!

Now he's fooling around taking time to get advice from this skinny little scout!" Tom smiled grimly. This was not going to be easy!

"Sergeant Tom Bluefoot."

"Sir."

"Come forward. I seek your advice regarding my plans for the Counsel. Stand at attention."

"Yes sir."

"How long have you been back here to Green Ville, Sergeant?"

Tom appreciated Wayne's emphasis on his newly acquired rank. "Since the middle of June sir," Tom replied, still at attention.

"At ease soldier. Then it must be apparent to you as it certainly is to me and these officers that this whole affair is taking far too long!" Everyone jumped as Wayne's fist slammed down on the table. "I am asking your advice, Tom Bluefoot." Looks of disgust appeared on two of the seated officers' faces.

"If I can be of any help, General, of course I . . ."

Wayne continued, glancing at each officer in turn. "I plan to round up all the chiefs who still have not had a chance to speak, as well as those who already have. The treaty document is ready and has been for a week! At my orders they will make their mark and get this over with! Your suggestions, Sergeant Bluefoot?"

"General Wayne and all officers here," Tom began courteously, "I must strongly caution against any such action. If you prevent even one of the chiefs from his rightful chance to make his speech, all may be lost!"

Major Brice jumped up and cried out, "What do you mean by such words? Apologize to the General!"

"Sit down Major," Wayne commanded "the scout is doing exactly as I asked. He meant no disrespect. It is my considered opinion that had we spent more time listening to the natives it might not be necessary to be doing any of what we find ourselves burdened with today. Now Tom, why do you say this?"

Confidently Tom spoke again. "Because Sir, my people are a proud people. Now they find themselves forced to accept whatever their conquerors decide to allow them. Only the chance to address this gathering can hope to replace at least a little of their lost dignity. Please hear me," here Tom looked at all the faces of the officers, "when I urge the utmost patience in these critical dealings with my people." While not really in respect, the officers did at least appear to consider what they had heard.

"Thank you Sergeant. Do you have anything else you wish to say?" Wayne asked.

"Only this, gentlemen. I am not an officer and I am certainly not a chief! I speak only as one of a conquered people. You, General Wayne, have the respect of the Indians gathered here. The main reason is because you have taken almost a year to gather all those in power over my people and given them opportunity to voice their concerns. Earlier treaties, I have been told, were not conducted in this way. Once again I urge you, take all the time necessary to hear each and every one's address. Do not lose your advantage by being impatient."

There was silence in the room for several minutes. "We will consider your advice, Sergeant. You can also be of further service. I will draw up an itinerary for all remaining chiefs. Find them and tell them of the time and date of their oration. Is that clear?"

"Yes General, but . . .but . . that is . . well I can't read very well, so . . ."

"Of course. Major Brice you will accompany the sergeant and do the necessary reading as he interprets."

"Me Sir? I'm to go with this here Indian, Sir?"

"Yes, you," Wayne said angrily. "Do you have a hearing problem, or is it a problem with taking and following simple orders? Your name is Brice is it not? Speak up, man!"

"Yes Sir, General! You can count on me and . . . and .. .him, Sir."

"Very good. That's all for this morning gentlemen. Dismissed."

*   *   *

Over a thousand Native Americans were gathered in the oak grove just over a mile from the fort. Most were seated, but a few resolute minor chiefs stood, ignoring the flies and mosquitoes that hovered over them. The officers of the Legion of America were seated at a series of rough tables and benches which had been serving for the nearly six weeks of proceedings. The day, August first, seventeen ninety-five, was hot and humid as only the weather could be in the middle of summer in this part of North America. The soldiers, buttoned to the chin in their dress uniforms, could not help but envy those Indians who were unclothed above the waist. It was remarkably quiet considering the huge glut of humanity under the oak trees. For various reasons most of the Native Americans did not speak.

Who could blame General Wayne and the other officers for their impatience? The proceedings had been going on for so long! Still there were many chiefs who had not yet had the opportunity to speak. In addition to the better known tribes, also in attendance were the Delaware, Ottawa, Chippewa, Potawatomie, Wea, Kaskaskia, Seneca, and even a few Septs whose leaders may or may not have been officially invited.

Such a diversity of languages and dialects had necessitated twelve additional translators. The process required for some of the sessions bordered on the comical, although the army contingent found little to laugh about! A native who could speak at least two languages would relay the words to another who would then pass them on to Tom Bluefoot, Blue Jacket, or another Indian who spoke some English.

Whether the original meaning or its intent actually made its way to the soldiers is highly unlikely. No one seemed to care however, as the chief had had his say and would sign the treaty when his opportunity came.

Little Turtle had purposefully delayed making his oration. Only Chief Blue Jacket's words remained to be heard on the following day.

Uncharacteristically, as Little Turtle, war chief of the Miami nation, mounted the platform of squared logs he raised both arms to the sky. "Oh Great Spirit," he began in a voice hardly audible to those on the fringes, "hear my words. May they be true and agreeable to all." Tom stood on the great chief's right, using a birch bark moose call as a megaphone. Blue Jacket, on Little Turtle's left nodded approval at Bluefoot's translation, but said nothing. "I am Michikinikwa, principal chief of the great Miami nation," he continued. "It is my land upon which we stand at this moment. For many days I had not planned to speak at the Mad General's Council of Peace. Then I knew that our people would need much wisdom to be sure that all tribes received a fair share of what was promised us for signing the large paper. For this reason I speak these words to you now."

"Observe the small Wyandot at my right hand." Tom nearly fainted when Little Turtle made mention of him. "He is a traitor to our people and served as a spy for the white man's army." Several soldiers leaped to their feet, expecting violence, but the chief continued, undisturbed. "He has claimed that his actions were done to bring a faster conclusion to the war, in order to save lives." After a lengthy pause he stated emphatically, "I believe him!"

Toom-She-chi-Kwa struggled with the translation, casting an eye at Blue Jacket as he did so. The Shawnee chief made no effort to disguise his contempt for Little Turtle's seeming endorsement of Tom's words.

Little Turtle continued, unperturbed. "All of this land," and he named the recognized boundaries, "have belonged to the Miami for longer than any one now living can remember. I and those great Miami chiefs who preceded me have never prevented other tribes from building their villages and planting their gardens in all of this good country. I speak for them as well as for those of my tribe." He went on.

Tom translated smoothly, converting the Chief's words into English. As soon as he had finished, Blue Jacket did the same for those tribes not familiar with the dialect of the Miami. In that manner the proceedings continued until late afternoon.

Showing virtually no fatigue after standing and speaking for several hours, Little Turtle left the makeshift platform and rejoined his warriors. Blue Jacket stalked off without a word to Tom or anyone else. Already the Shawnee chief was composing the oration he would make on the following day. It would not be as benign as the words of Little Turtle!

Gratefully, General Wayne and the other officers headed toward their barracks in Fort Green Ville. "One more day," the General sighed to his companions. "Blue Jacket will harangue us for a few hours, then we present the document. Call Tom Bluefoot if you please."

"Sir!"

Tom reported quickly.

"Sergeant Bluefoot, our thanks for your efforts as our main interpreter. How long have you been engaged in this activity?"

Tom was obviously exhausted. "I believe it has been more than twenty sessions, General. At times I was unsure if my voice would hold out. I am sorry that I was unable to be of help when the Kickapoo holy man spoke. Their language is too different from those I know."

"That was not a problem, Sergeant Bluefoot. That old fool rambled on so long that even his own tribesmen were falling asleep! Who was the other interpreter you found to help?"

"He is called 'Makes Way'. Although quite young, he speaks many languages of our people. He is a good man."

The General's gout had not been so bad during the weeks of the Grand Council, probably because he had been seated most of the time. He rose, stretched, then spoke to Tom again.

"I seek your advice once more, Sergeant," he began, "It seems that your people put great store in proper protocol. All things considered, I believe that so far the proceedings have gone very well. It would be more than foolish if I were to cause problems at this late date. Day after tomorrow I plan to present the treaty document for the Chiefs to make their marks. What should be the proper order as I call each one for his signature?"

"Do not call them!" Tom answered quickly. "This, the last official action most of them will take, must be by their own will. Thou wilt see that there will be little confusion as they come forward to sign. Each one is well aware of his standing at this gathering. Those of lessor rank or prestige will honor those above them by deferring to them. Chiefs of greatest power will be last to sign. You saw this demonstrated in the order by which they chose to make their speeches to the entire assembly over these last weeks. Please attend to my advice in this matter, General. Believe me, it is of great importance!"

Wayne smiled and glanced at the officers present. "Do you see why I put such store in this Wyandot Indian?" he asked. "I believe that he has done as much as anyone to ensure a peaceful and productive resolution to the entire endeavor! Again, my thanks Tom Bluefoot. You are dismissed."

Tom hadn't had a chance to eat all day. He hurried to the mess tent and presented his plate for a portion of beef and potatoes. He paid no attention to those standing in line with him. Their looks and cruel remarks no longer bothered the Wyandot. "You get lost, Injun? This is the army mess tent. Go get your vittles with the rest of your kind. You ain't wanted here! Go on before I call the sergeant and get you throwed out!"

Carefully balancing his plate, Tom turned and looked full in the face of the soldier. "You need not call a sergeant, corporal," Tom stated calmly, emphasizing the soldier's inferior rank. "As you can see," he tapped the stripes on his tunic, "I am a sergeant!"

"Better watch what you say, Porter," the man next in line whispered. "He's a interpretator for the officers! I seen him sittin' right there with 'em!"

"That don't cut no ice with me!" the corporal blustered, but everyone laughed as they watched him slink away, his plate only half full.

After eating alone at one of the tables, Tom set off to find Sean O'Casey. He had been too busy to see his friend for several weeks.

As usual, the surgeon's tent was practically overflowing. Soldiers waited in line or sat in the shade nearby, two with bandages prominently displayed. "Hey Tom! That you?" Sean yelled as he stripped a blood-stained bandage from a man's upper arm. The battle had happened well over a year before, but a few wounds continued to fester, and the sick were always in need of attention. "Be with you in a minute. Chloe, put a new bandage on this man's arm. Wash the wound off first though. We just can't seem to get this arrow wound to heal right. Does it still smell bad? Better get a bucket of fresh water first. This one's about half blood! Go upstream a ways before you get the water. The Senecas have been watering their horses downstream. Be careful you don't scoop up no crawdads when you dip the bucket in! Ha ha"

Sean's sleeves were rolled to his elbows. His apron had once been white, but was far from it by now! The redhead was obviously very tired, but Tom was happy to see how proud his friend appeared. It was more than simply pride in his work with the physician. A certain sparkle in his only eye and a sort of lopsided grin indicated that the Irishman was enjoying a secret of some kind.

"Tom," Sean said a little sheepishly, "you've met Chloe before haven't you?"

"Sure I have. Hello Chloe. How are you two getting along helping the surgeon? Still plenty to do, I'm sure."

Chloe stepped up behind Sean, but hadn't yet spoken. "The truth is, Tom," Sean said, moving one foot around in the dust, "Chloe and me are getting along real good! Isn't that right sweetie?"

Chloe's grin seemed to light up the whole area. "We sure are Tom! Sean here has asked me to marry him. It'd be legal too, since my Emil got killed in the battle last year."

"Emil? Who's Emil?" Tom asked, trying to get his mind around all this momentous news.

"He was my husband Emil was. He was one of them that the soldiers called 'sharpshooters'. He was a wonder with a rifle just like Big Cas was. We were only married a couple months but he kept us in fresh meat all the time. He'd sneak out away from the army in the evenings and hunt. I'd clean and dress out whatever he brought in and we'd have a feast! Usually there was enough left to share with his tent mates."

"How in the world could he get away with doing that? Surely some officer must have known what was going on. Couldn't they hear the shots?"

"Sure they could," Sean piped up. "But according to Chloe here, her husband always made sure that a good cut of meat went to the men in charge. Nobody ever gave him trouble over his hunting, but they made mighty certain that the General never heard about it!"

"A good man was my husband Emil," Chloe continued wistfully, "but Sean here is just as good or better. We aim to make a go of it. I know everything is going to be just fine. It sure ain't going to be like it was with them other two!"

Tom had hardly had a moment to say anything, but now he spoke up. "What do you mean 'the other two'?"

"Why my first two husbands of course. Chester and Sam their names was. Chester was a drunk. He beat me pretty regular, so I left him and married up with Sam. He was not a bad sort. Worked in a grist mill, but he went and got sick and kicked the bucket after we was only married a year or so. Sean," she said coyly, taking his arm, "is better than any of 'em even if he does have only one eye!"

Sean said nothing, but stood there with a sort of silly grin on his face.

"Even with all of them three, I never had no children," Chloe prattled on. "Me and Sean intends to correct that, don't we Sean?"

Sean's face turned almost as red as his hair. "Well we . . .uh . . . I reckon that . . ." he looked around desperately for the surgeon, hoping to be called back to work before much more of this talk could go on.

Tom grabbed Sean by the arm and literally dragged him several paces away. "Sean are you sure about this? Do you really plan to marry this woman?" he whispered.

"Yes I do!" Sean replied emphatically. "Why shouldn't I?"

"Well for one thing she's got to be six or eight years older than you. Have you thought about that?"

"Ten!" Sean almost shouted.

"What do you mean?"

"She's ten years older than me, and I don't care. We're going to get married next month when my enlistment's up."

"But Sean she's had three husbands already! You'd be number four. Doesn't that bother you a little? And there's another thing that . ."

Sean's Irish temper was about to boil over. "So what's the 'other thing'?" he asked, plainly angry.

"Take it easy Sean. We've been friends for a long time. We've been through a lot together, and we're still going to be friends, but just listen for a minute."

"Well go ahead," Sean snapped. "Chloe and I have to be getting back to work."

"Hey, don't get mad! What I'm afraid of is that you haven't really considered who this woman is. She's nothing but a camp follower Sean. You know that none of them are any good. Not to be married at least!"

"I've worked with Chloe for almost two years. You get to know a person real well when you work side-by-side with them every day. Now you say, 'none of the camp followers are any good'. You, of all people, should see that this is no different than what a lot of people keep saying about Indians like you! You're sure to have heard people, especially Big Cas, saying 'the only good Indian is a dead Indian' haven't you? Remember how Caswell tried to kill you just because you are an Indian? That led to your 'desertion', the floggings, and everything. By the time he really got to know you he could see that you were as good as anybody, and better than most!"

Tom caught him by the arm again. "Thou art surely right, Sean. People judge me because I am a 'redskin' no matter what kind of man I really am. I'm very sorry Sean. Forgive me, can you?"

"Well o.k., but I've heard all of this kind of talk before and I'm not interested in any more of it!"

"Tell you what Sean," Tom said, still holding onto his friend's arm, "I'll be your 'best man' if I'm still here when you two get hitched."

"Thanks Tom, but Captain Friederich has already offered to do that for us. Maybe the wedding will be held in Pittsburgh where we plan to live. Anyway no hard feelings! You're still the best friend I'll ever have!"

"Come back here, O'Casey! Where you been anyway?" the surgeon shouted.

With a nonchalant grin, Sean answered carelessly, "We'll be back in a minute. I'm not deserting!"

The friends shook hands in the Indian fashion, gripping forearms. "Haven't seen you in quite a while Tom. I hear you been real busy with the translating. How's that going?"

"Pretty well I think. Can you believe it, one more day then the signing starts. Sure hope that goes well."

"It will. Don't worry," Sean stated, ignoring the Captain's angry looks. "I hear you and the General are real pals these days. Is that the way it is?"

Tom grinned at his friend. "I'm afraid not Sean, but he seems satisfied with what I've been doing. I guess my part will be pretty much over after the signing is done."

'What do you plan to do then? Are you going to stay in the army?"

Toom-she-chi-Kwa didn't answer for a minute. "Really I don't know," he said finally. "Nobody has offered to keep me on. Won't be much need for a scout anymore I guess. A lot of my people are heading west. Some will probably go on beyond the big river they call 'The

Father of Waters'. They think the settlers will never go that far, so they will be left in peace. I've thought some about maybe going out that way myself. What do you think?"

"You Indians are just fooling yourselves. You know as well as I do that the settlers will eventually go there too. First the trappers and traders, then the homesteaders. There will be trouble. And do you know who will be sent out there then?"

"The army I suppose. Some of the chiefs said the same thing when they made their speeches at the fort." Tom answered ruefully. "You're right Sean, but maybe a man like me, sort of half one way and half the other, could help keep things from getting too bloody out there. Sometimes I wish . . ."

"Sean O'Casey! Get back here! I'm ready to take the bullet out of the Lieutenant. Chloe's here already. I need your help! Hurry up!"

Sean shook his head as he stood and dusted off his pants. "Got to go, Tom. You heard the Captain. Listen, before you go anywhere, come and find me. If the army has moved on, come to Pittsburgh some time. Find the Captain's doctor office. Chloe and I will probably be there. So long, my friend. Remember . . ."

"Right now!" the surgeon yelled. Sean trotted off, calling to Chloe that he was coming.

"So long, Sean. I'll find you . . . some time." Tom sat back down, sad to think this might be the last time he would ever be able to talk with his friend, but he realized that life sometimes took such turns.

* * *

The word had spread! Blue Jacket, chief of the Kispokotha sect of the Shawnee Nation, was preparing to address the Great Council of Peace. His would be the final oration before the signing would take place on the following day, August third, 1795.

"I am Blue Jacket of the Shawnee!" he began in a voice that carried well, even to the most distance listeners. Tom had all he could do to keep up with the Indian's words.

There was much anticipation and curiosity about the substance of the words he would speak. "Brothers! I speak from inside me, here." He thumped his remarkable chest and almost glared at the seated officers. Turning slightly in their direction he continued. "You are white men. Your fine cloaks, fancy hats, and trousers the color of doeskin do not completely cover the color of your skin. I am sure that most of you know that I too was once of that pale color. Not any more!" These words were nothing less than a shout! Turning once more toward the masses of Indian listeners, he said, "I have thrown away [here he made a slashing motion with one hand] all that was once my past life. Now I am wholly and completely of the people!" A rumbling of angry agreement rolled from the crowded listeners. One of Wayne's officers rose halfway from his bench, but with a look the General indicated that he remain seated.

"I, whom you Americans call Blue Jacket, have led our warriors to glorious victories. There would have been another such triumph had the treacherous British and Canadians kept their promises of help. Pah! Now I must walk a different path. Those seated there," he indicated the officers with a sweep of one arm, "are promising that all who make their mark on the yellow paper tomorrow are to receive presents. Not only such presents as blankets, tools, and the worthless white man's clothing, but payments of silver money with which we may buy more. Furthermore, these silver monies are to be given to each of our tribes for many years to come." He turned completely around until he faced the officers directly. "Are my words correct? Do I speak the truth?" He waited until the General had heard the complete translation. Finally Wayne stood, nodding in agreement. "Then so be it! I will take the trail of peace with the whites. That is, so long as they are made to obey the rules agreed to in this Grand Council of Peace."

"As many here very well know, I was born in Pennsylvania. With thirteen brothers and sisters I was left alone much of the time. Befriended by an aging Indian, I learned the ways of the warrior and the mysteries of the forests. I was sickened by your people's [he glared at the officers again] treatment of the tribes who were the real owners of the land, even that upon which we find ourselves. I left the white man's world for a better life among my red brothers."

Tom's arm was getting stiff from holding the megaphone, but he persevered, translating as rapidly as clear speech allowed. Blue Jacket remained standing, impassive to the reactions of the listeners, both red and white.

"It was not that long ago that as a young man of twenty winters I was part of our victory at Point Pleasant. Then four years ago I was war chief when we faced and defeated St. Claire's army. Those who were there saw my courage and cunning. I was promoted for my prowess."

"Listen to that durn redskin!" one of the officers growled. "Give 'em a chance to talk and they'll tell you everything they ever done. Bragging is all they know. It makes me sick!"

Major Scott spoke up in reply. "Tom Bluefoot told me that they do that because they want to influence the youngsters to be brave. With no written language, they have to be sure that their deeds are noticed. It's their way of encouraging the young."

"So that there Injun told you that did he? General Wayne better quit listening to him all the time. He'll get to be a 'Injun lover' like some other officers I could name!" He flicked an openly accusatory look at the Major.

"If I were you," Major Scott replied calmly, "I'd be careful about criticizing General Wayne. He doesn't take kindly to being second guessed!"

The latest translation completed, Blue Jacket resumed his speech.

"It is my pleasure to compliment the white men Daniel Boone and Simon Kenton. Although they were enemies of my people, they showed courage and resourcefulness. Their dealings with us were mostly fair, so I know there are good Shemanese among the whites."

Tom's voice had finally given out completely. General Wayne strode forward and declared a recess in the proceedings until Toom-She-chi-Kwa could overcome a fit of coughing. Offered a bench by one of the officers, Blue Jacket declined. He remained standing, arms folded and head erect. He cast a disdainful glance at Tom, considering the recess a disgusting example of a lack of stamina. For a moment the chief had forgotten that the interpreter was an Indian. A Wyandot!

"What will become of my wife, 'The Swan', and my daughter and son now that the so-called Peace Treaty will become the law for both red man and white? What will this mean for our young men who must hunt for the deer, the elk, and the bear? Will those who will now be allowed to build their cabins and grow their crops build fences as they have always done in the past? Will the animals and birds given to us by the 'Great Spirit', Gitchie Manitou, run far from this land? Will hunting become so poor that many will die of hunger? These thoughts are mine, but not mine alone. Every chief and medicine man has the same concerns!"

General Wayne asked Tom if he was able to continue. After a drink of water from a tin cup, Tom assured him that he would have no further problem. When this latest, lengthy interpretation was concluded, Blue Jacket, who after all spoke English too, nodded gravely in agreement.

"My words are over!"

There was shocked silence. No one expected his words to last less than an hour.

Little Turtle was gone. He had left just before Blue Jacket began his oration. This insult proved that the two major chiefs were becoming enemies.

"Sergeant Bluefoot. Report to the General's headquarters."

"Thank you sir. He had come to feel that Wayne was almost his friend. He would have been heartbroken if he'd known the great man would be dead of his illnesses in less than two years.

He headed to the surgeon's tents. "Where's O'Casey?" he asked.

"You just missed him. He Said if you came by to tell you he'd be back in about a week. Went for more medicine. Maybe you could take his place."

"No thanks! I wouldn't last a day in this kind of work!" He headed for headquarters.

"Sit down Sergeant Bluefoot. How do you feel the final orations went?"

"All went well, but you should be aware that Little Turtle and Blue Jacket are becoming enemies."

"That may become significant in the coming years. Now as to yourself. You must be aware that the scouts are being dismissed. Did you receive you wages?"

"Yes Sir. Thank you Sir."

"One more thing." Wayne opened a drawer on his battered campaign desk. He took out a small item, about the size of the former scout's palm. He stood, cleared his throat, and formally presented Toom-She-chi-Kwa with a solid silver Medal Of Peace!

*   *   *

Toom-She-chi-Kwa kept the peace medal out of sight as he passed the mess tent. He carried the musket the quartermaster had given him, but the nasty and suspicious looks by the cooks discouraged him from entering. He was not hungry anyway.

The now unemployed scout wandered into the forest, stopping when he found a small, quiet glade.

“I sure wish Sean was here,” he thought miserably. “Or even Chloe. Sure would be nice to have somebody nice to talk to. The truth is I don’t have any idea of what I should do now.”

A squirrel crept down the side of an elm tree, chattering angrily at the seated Indian. “So even you won’t talk to me, eh? Well I’m not surprised. Go on back where you belong!” He threw a pine cone at the animal but it merely flicked its tail and continued its harangue. “I’m pretty sure I know what Sean would tell me,” he thought. “He’d say go on back to Pennsylvania and find that Quaker who raised you. He’d probably be glad to have you back again since your father is dead now.”

Tom remembered his Quaker "father" fondly, and for a moment considered returning to the home he had once known. "But," he thought sadly, "it's been over eight years since I last saw him. He may no longer be living, or he may have moved away. Besides," he told himself, "at his age he might not welcome an Indian, now a grown man, re-entering his life. No, I won't try to find him again." The squirrel chattered a moment, then scampered up the tree and out of sight. Tom was alone again!

His mind finally made up, Toom-she-chi-Kwa used a little of his back pay to provision a traveling kit. He sold the musket to a homesteader he met, feeling that carrying the weapon would cause distrust and suspicion by those whom he might meet on his journey. Without the gun he would be unable to hunt, but he was well aware that he had little skill in the forest, and virtually none with a firearm. It was a heavy piece and he was happy to be rid of it.

Tom had no problem deciding where to go. As a Wyandot, even one now hated and considered a traitor by many of his tribe, anyone still left at Roundhead's village would be obligated by protocol to accept him.

The former scout had never been to Roundhead's village. He knew it was made up of many "longhouses", each of which could contain as many as five or six families. Whether he might be asked to make his home in one of these he had no idea. It was a frightening thought!

The journey could take as long as two weeks, depending on what help he could get on the way. The rivers provided the fastest and safest mode of travel, but Tom had no experience manipulating a birchbark canoe, even if he could buy one. Still he knew he must learn and learn quickly, as the fall rains were already causing the smaller creeks to rise.

With many misgivings Tom approached a young adventurer who had established a trading post on the nearby Stillwater River. Business had not been good, due to tensions and uncertainty during negotiations with the tribes during the recently completed Council of Peace. He was surprised to find himself dealing with an Indian who had real money.

"Well Injun, I do happen to have a canoe for sale. Just what you need too! It was made by an Ottawa who used it when he was trapping beaver. She's light as a feather and don't leak a drop neither! There it is, upside down back of that shed."

Tom was appalled. Although it appeared to be in good condition it was so small! The trader was right about the weight. The man picked it up and easily hoisted it over his head. He dropped it into the shallows and pointed proudly at the way it floated, hardly settling at all. "You don't look like you've got much gear, and if I can say so, you ain't very big yourself. This here's just right for you, no matter where you plan to go. Hop in. Try her out. Here's a paddle."

Gingerly, tom stepped into the tiny craft. His weight lifted the bow and he was suddenly afloat. Trying to settle himself caused the canoe to flip over, dumping Tom into the river. Floundering around in the knee-deep water, Toom-she-chi-Kwa promptly managed to poke one foot through the canoe's bark side. Dripping and embarrassed, he dragged the water filled canoe back onto the bank.

"What in tarnation happened?" the trader growled. "You should have waited for me to give you instructions about canoes! Well kid, looks like you just done bought yourself a canoe!"

"But it's got a hole in it!" Tom cried.

"Yeah, I can see that," he replied sarcastically. "Now it's going to cost you four bits more than my first price."

"More?" Tom yelled. "Why should it cost more now?"

"Cause I'm gonna charge you for patching the hole you made! That's why. Now hand over the money."

After a two day wait for the pine sap "glue" to dry, a price was agreed upon. The repair completed, Tom could finally paddle cautiously away, learning as he went.

Light as it admittedly was, the Indian had all he could do to carry it and his kit on the several "portages" necessary to get from river to river and keep heading in the right direction.

Long before he could see the palisade around Roundhead's village, Tom had been observed by women and children busy along the river. He kept on paddling, smiling and waving in a friendly fashion.

Nearing the village he was "escorted" ashore by three well-muscled braves who seemed anything but happy to see him.

"Who are you and what are you doing here?" one of the men asked with a scowl. They held the canoe near the bank as Tom climbed out.

"I am Toom-She-chi-Kwa, a Wyandot like yourselves. I am to be welcomed by Chief Roundhead, who will undoubtedly remember me as one of the interpreters at the Great Council of Peace in Green Ville."

"Oh yes, he will recognize you! I myself recognize you! A traitor to your own people. A manipulator of all the chiefs' words in favor of the soldiers. We will take you to Chief Roundhead, but you will be lucky if he doesn't order that you be killed and your head impaled on a pole! Come with us if you dare."

Tom stood erect, expanded his skinny chest and lifted his chin. "I am not afraid of your threats. My good friend, the Mad General himself has assured me that should I come to harm he will send a whole regiment of soldiers to kill your braves and burn your lodges to the ground!" Wayne had made no such promises of course!

One of the three laughed at such arrogant words, but the other two pulled him a short distance away. "We must be cautious about this," one of them whispered. "I can assure you that this fool is a friend of the American General. I saw how he was treated during the Peace Council. General Wayne himself brought him a cup of water when he had trouble speaking. Didn't you two see that?" Stealing glances at the scout, they finally agreed that they had.

Roundhead rudely ignored the small Indian standing humbly inside the door of his longhouse. He pretended to give special attention to a small tear in his elegant leggings. Finally he looked up and spoke. "What is it that brings you here to our village? I must tell you now that you are not welcome here! Surely one intelligent enough to be an interpreter for the murdering soldier calling himself 'mad' must not be surprised by our hatred for a traitor such as you!"

Tom was shocked. He had considered the fact that there would be enemies in the Indian camps, but he had not expected it from Chief Roundhead, who was known as a fair and wise leader. Still he managed to compose himself and reply. "I can certainly understand your feelings, great Chief," he began humbly, "but if I may have your attention for but a few minutes I will . . ."

"Enough! Speak no further until I invite another Wyandot chief and a personal friend of mine to hear whatever you have to say, useless though it may be." He clapped twice and a brave appeared in the doorway. "Find Chief Tarhe," he commanded. "Ask him to join us for an important meeting. He is probably at the longhouse of Chickisawa. Hurry!"

Tarhe, "The Crane", had been invited to Roundhead's village several days before. Known as one who had been doing all he could to improve relations between the red men and the whites, he now proved to be Tom's deliverer. He made an impassioned speech in Tom's behalf reminding Roundhead that even the great chief Little Turtle had publicly defended Toom-she-chi-Kwa at the treaty signing proceedings.

Tom breathed a great sigh of relief, and thanked The Crane effusively.

After considerable talk, during which Tom was mostly silent, Roundhead spoke his final words. "It is only my great respect for the wisdom of my friend, Tarhe, that I agree to see to your safety. However my advice to you would be that you be in your canoe and gone before the moon is high tonight. I will give an order that you are not to be harmed, but some of the young braves may not obey."

Tarhe surprised young Tom by placing one hand on his shoulder. "I will get word to all I can that you are not to be molested, no matter where you go. Like Little Turtle, I agree that your intentions were for the purpose of saving lives, regardless of whether Indian or white. Go in Peace!"

Ignoring Roundhead's warning, Tom could not help swaggering a little as he walked to the river. A small crowd, among them the three braves who had first accosted him, watched in silence as the small Wyandot, accompanied by The Crane, launched his canoe and paddled calmly away.

*   *   *

Two weeks later Tom was again at Fort Green Ville, alone and discouraged. Their enlistment times now up, Captain Friederich, Sean, and Chloe were gone, probably to Pittsburgh. A few recruits still manned the fort, but they mostly ignored Tom, who wandered disconsolately around the area, still undecided about his future.

Attempting to talk with the two officers left in charge at the fort, he was angrily rebuffed. With General Wayne no longer present to defend him they were not interested in the problems of a single Wyandot Indian! Hatred and distrust of the "redskins" would continue for generations to come.

Toward evening three days later, two soldiers, one younger and smaller, called him to their campfire.

"Hey Injun," one of the soldiers began, "Ain't you the one who did the talking so us soldiers could tell what the chiefs were saying?"

"I did some of it," Tom replied shortly. There was something about the two that caused him to wonder. Why were they lying around, not even near the other recruits, and well away from the fort?

"Sure I remember you alright! Why you just stood up on that platform and called out the words in English. Right in front of the General and them other officers too. Wasn't you scared?"

Both soldiers were smiling in a kindly manner. When the older one asked him to sit down and have some hot cornmeal mush he agreed at once.

They were just what the scout needed at this time. Someone to talk with! By asking questions and encouraging him to speak up, they soon learned all about Tom's life. They seemed impressed, but shared little about their own lives.

As the small fire burned down to glowing coals, the younger soldier said he was going to sleep. With hardly another word he rolled up in his blanket and stretched out, feet to the fire. His friend lit a small pipe and puffed away until he had it drawing well. Leaning back against a log he unhooked the canteen from his belt and shook it gently.

"Me, I aim to have a drink before I curl up. Want a snort?"

Tom shook his head, visions of his drunken father filling his head.

"Aw come on Bluefoot. I don't like to drink alone and my partner here is snoring away already. Don't you Injuns like a little whiskey now and then?"

"Thank you friend, but I've seen what strong drink has done to some of our people. I better not, but you go ahead."

The older soldier smiled as he extended the canteen toward Tom's face. "Hey, lookee here, Bluefoot. I don't mean for you to have more than a sip or two, just to be friendly. Besides this is all I got and no chance to get any more that I know of. Go ahead, just take a swaller or two."

Grateful for their friendship, and not wanting to be impolite, he accepted the vessel and took a sip. Although it burned his throat, he was amazed at how soon it made him feel happy and at peace. "I can certainly see how this had been so appealing to my father and many like him," he thought.

"Go ahead, have another," his friend said after taking a drink himself.

The early fall night suddenly seemed almost too warm. Tom remembered stretching out beside the first soldier, a contented smile on his face.

Finally waking to full daylight, Toom-She-chi-Kwa struggled to sit up, his head pounding. The fire pit was laced with cold ashes.

Both soldiers were gone!

In short order Tom discovered that not only were his "friends" nowhere to be seen, but his shirt and army issue boots were missing as well! Panic struck him then. With growing dread he emptied his possibles bag. It was gone! His silver peace medal, the one he had kept hidden in the bottom of his kit, the one presented to him by General Wayne himself, had been stolen!

"What a fool I have been!" Tom groaned aloud. "I of all people should have known what whiskey can do. I will never use the devil drink again!"

He made it to the creek before vomiting repeatedly. Plunging his face and head into the cool water, he began to feel a little better. After resting for a time he stood up. The whole world seemed to be whirling round and round. He sat or collapsed to the ground and finally fell into a fitful, dream-ridden slumber.

Toom-She-chi-Kwa didn't know he was dreaming. Everything seemed so real! Half hidden in a feathery fog, a figure slowly appeared. Tom recognized him immediately. It was Black Pipe!

"Is it really you, my uncle? How I had wished for your wisdom and counsel during these last three years. You had last appeared to me when I was in peril, afraid of the soldier, Big Cas. Did you know that he and I became friends? Sergeant Caswell died a hero in the battle by the jumbled trees." Tom was almost sputtering in his eagerness to address the apparition.

"You have done well," Black Pipe said quietly.

"Oh my uncle, I am in need of your advice!" Black Pipe's image seemed to be growing fainter. "Do not leave me! Not yet! What shall I do now? How am I to spend my remaining days?"

"When you awake, look carefully at you own image reflected in the pool near your feet." Black Pipe said clearly. "You will see yourself! That is all you have been thinking of. You have asked yourself if the Quaker would welcome you back. What of the old man himself? His wife having died years ago, he has been alone since your father took you from him. He is old and all alone. He needs the help of a man who is young and strong. A man who loves him. Go to him. Be a son to him once more. I have spoken."

Tom was suddenly jerked wide awake by a hard kick in the side. A soldier stood over him, ready to kick him again. "Get up and get away from the fort," he growled. "You ain't nothing but a drunken red Indian!

I ought to shoot you and rid the world of another 'whiskey Indian'! Get going before I do it!"

Tom jumped up, ignoring his pounding head and smiled brightly. "Thank you, Private!" He said, grinning. The soldier stared in astonishment as Toom-She-chi-Kwa trotted away, laughing aloud.

That night, his mind clear and his purpose decided, Tom prepared his few belongings and curled up to sleep under a beech tree far from the fort.

I'll head east on the Ohio," he told himself. "My canoe will take me. So long as I don't stick my foot through it again! If my Quaker father has died or cannot be found I'll try to locate Doctor Friederich and the newlyweds. After that I'll just have to see what happens."

"Somewhere in this land, perhaps beyond the Mississippi, there must be a need for a Wyandot interpreter. May Gitchie Manitou protect me!"

He slept the sleep of the pure in heart.

THE END

AVAILABLE SOON:

BOOK TWO

"Tom Bluefoot, Chief Tecumseh, and the War of 1812"

About the Author

Lloyd Harnishfeger retired after thirty-seven years in public education. He was a teacher, principal, and then, for twenty years, was a curriculum director for Putnam County, Ohio, schools. He was named Outstanding Supervisor by the Ohio Association of School Supervisors and Outstanding Alumnus at Bluffton College, his alma mater. Lloyd has authored nine books, several of these dealing with the teaching of "listening skills" to public schoolchildren. They are in use all over the United States as well as in several foreign countries. His lifelong avocation is the collection and study of American Indian artifacts, which led to the subject of most of his published books.

Lloyd lives in Pandora, Ohio, with his wife of fifty-nine years. Marjorie is a retired public school music teacher. Their daughter Rebecca is chairperson of the music department at Ohio Northern University.